AQUA CI

Part Two

Deeper Than Yesterday

by James David

Illustrated by Rex Aldred and James David

MOONBEAM

To Mia
Best Wishes
James David

First Published in the United Kingdom in 2004
by Moonbeam Publishing
Reprinted 2010

ISBN No. 0-9547704-1-2
EAN No. 978-0954 770419

Bibliographical Data Services
British Library Cataloguing-in-Publication Data
A catalogue record for this book is available
from the British Library

**acknowledgement of permission to include
print of archive postcard of Sandsend
Judges Postcards Ltd., St. Leonards-on-Sea,
East Sussex, TN38 8BN (01424 438538)**

Printed and bound by:
The Max Design & Print Co
Kettlestring Lane, Clifton Moor,
York YO30 4XF

AQUA CRYSTA

To
Poppy, Basil, Jacko, Spicy, Podge, Munchkins, Jack, Tiny, Jet, Norris, Scamp, Tanya, Bungle, Rosie, Meg, Mouse, Tack and Daisy
all the dogs we fostered
for the wonderful Whitby Dog Rescue
and who all found loving homes

AQUA CRYSTA

Part 2

Deeper Than Yesterday

Chapter 1

Silence...just silence...as deep and solid as silence could ever be...filled the blackness of the winter's night.

Not a single sound could be heard.

Nor was there the faintest breath of wind.

But it was cold.

Very cold!

All the creatures of the forest, even those of the moon hours, were tucked away from the threatening chill. Not a single paw print blemished the smooth, white blanket of snow that clothed the once green track that lead from the moor road to the Forest-Keeper's cottage, now called *Deer Leap*.

The snug, stone built cottage nestled just off the steadily

whitening corridor through the trees, about a quarter of a mile from the road. It was surrounded by tall, evergreen spruce, each one already heavily laden with snow.

Deer Leap's roof was white, too, as was the whole of the vast pine plantation which the children of the cottage had christened *George* back in the warmth of late summer.

Feathery flakes of snow fell noiselessly through a pale, red glow which was cast into the cold darkness by the lights of a Christmas tree in one of the cottage's downstairs windows. Here, the pink tinged, sugary white deepened secretly as the cottage peacefully slept and the embers of its living room fire died.

All was quiet on this silent night...on this night of nights...the magical night between Christmas Eve and Christmas Day...without doubt, the most enchanting night of the year!

But it has to be said that these particular brands of magic were of nothing compared to the wicked sorcery which was brewing deep, deep beneath the fallen snow of the sleeping forest that winter's night. For deep in the depths of the rocks below the *Harvestlands,* an evil plot had been hatched by a certain individual who sought power over the secret, timeless kingdom known as *Aqua Crysta* - the magical realm discovered by the children of the cottage just a short, few months before.

Then, it had been *'good magic'* that had drawn Jessica and her younger brother, Jamie, into the forest they called *George*...and threats from the Upper World had been seen off...but now, it was a totally different matter!

The threat came from within *Aqua Crysta* itself!

A traitor was at work! And his scheming plan was about to bear fruit!

As a crowd of bewildered Aqua Crystans gathered in glum silence in the *Meeting Hall Cavern* by the River Floss, just north of the Island of Galdo, Tregarth glanced with an evil smile at his two fellow conspirators. He had already addressed anxious crowds in the townships of Pillo, Middle Floss and even Galdo...this last

2

meeting defiantly within a crystal's throw of Queen Venetia's Palace itself!

But this gathering, in the vast, glistening amphitheatre of the *Meeting Hall,* would be the one that finally persuaded the Queen that it was time for her reign to end...and that it was time for a new King to sit upon the *Elmwood and Crystal Throne*!

Meanwhile, unknown to the inhabitants of the secret realm of *Aqua Crysta,* way above their heads, the snow continued to fall and bury their ancient Harvestlands. The snow grew deeper and the cold grew colder. And the only sound to be heard was the measured 'tick...tock... tick...tock' of the old grandfather clock in *Deer Leap's* hallway.

Suddenly, the silence of the cottage was shattered by an eerie, ghostly creak.

It came from the stairs...the third step down to be precise!

"Sssh, Jess, or dad'll hear us!" whispered Jamie, annoyed with his sister for not remembering the noisy third step, especially on this most important of missions.

Soundlessly, they crept down the rest of the stairs, opened the living-room door and tip-toed over to the Christmas tree in the window.

During the last few days they had decorated it with coloured baubles, tinsel, bells and lights. Their father loved Christmas and he insisted on a packed tree almost groaning under its load. Laid beneath was a jumble of colourfully wrapped shapes - presents from dad to Jessica and Jamie - which Jessica guessed he must have placed secretly after they had gone to bed.

"Wowee!" burst Jamie in as loud a whisper as he dared. "Looks as though Santa's been already!"

"He has!" whispered Jessica, who was two years older than her brother.

"Look at the mantelpiece! The sherry glass is empty!"

"And the mince pies have gone!" gasped Jamie. Being nine years old, his belief in Santa Claus was still as strong as ever, but his sister was beginning to have secret doubts which, of course, she kept to herself. "Let's put dad's presents under the tree and get back to bed," she whispered as she crept behind the settee where they'd hidden them. Without a sound, they quickly placed the four wrapped gifts with the others and then Jessica tip-toed to the door ready for the return journey to bed. She looked over her shoulder expecting Jamie to be behind her, but instead he was gazing out of the window by the tree, frantically waving his arms, beckoning her to join him.

"Come on!" Jessica whispered. "You promised you'd go back to bed as soon as we'd finished!"

"But, Jess, come and look at this!" Jamie insisted. "It's snowing!"

Jessica tip-toed back over to the window and her face beamed as she, too, looked through the window. The pale pink snowflakes falling through the light from the Christmas tree was a magical sight. They both stared, enchanted, and thoughts of the other magic of the forest flashed through their minds.

Right from the start, back in the last days of August, when they had first arrived in the forest, *George* had shared its greatest secret with the children. They had discovered its ancient stone walls with their mysterious tiny treasures, which had lead them to the ruins of Old Soulsyke Farm, and its well and the magical forest cellar. The adventure had always seemed like a dream in which they had met the people who lived in the timeless, shrunken world of *Aqua Crysta* beneath the well. There they had met Queen Venetia, Mayor Merrick, Lepho, Quentin and Toby and, most special of all, Jonathan and Jane.

They had sailed upon the River Floss in the 'Goldcrest' and visited the townships of Galdo and Pillo. They had marvelled at the clockwork toys of the forest cellar or *'The Palace of Dancing Horses'* as the Aqua Crystans called it. They had often thought of Jonathan and Jane, the two children who had once lived at Old

Soulsyke Farm until their nasty uncle had been forced to abandon it when the forest had been planted half a century ago. The two children had run away to *Aqua Crysta* and now lived in Pillo, but they were still the same age, now, fifty years later! That was the real magic - the agelessness of the place, where time stood still...something to do with the bubbly, frothy water that gushed from deep beneath the enchanted realm and flowed through the crystal cavern from one end to the other and then back again!

The silent snow continued to fall and the whiteness beyond the cottage window became deeper and deeper. As Jessica and Jamie stared into the trees across the track, the same thoughts, as usual, filled their minds. The snow, after all, was very tempting...and, it was the first of the winter...and the first they'd known since moving to the Yorkshire Moors.

"Jess," whispered Jamie, "how about...?"

"...Going out in the snow?" Jessica finished.

Jamie nodded and they both smiled.

"But how can we go outside at one o'clock on the night before Christmas?" asked Jessica. "Nobody's out at this time. Everyone's in bed dreaming of Christmas Day. It's not the thing to do, and, besides, we've only got our pyjamas on! It'll be freezing out there!"

"Oh, come on, Jess!" urged Jamie. "All we need are our thick, woolly pullies, our scarves, waterproofs and wellies...and they're all in the back porch!"

Without another word, they both darted on tip-toes through into the kitchen and into the porch... and, in a swirl of excitement they pulled on their outdoor clothes over their pyjamas.

A couple of minutes later they were stepping out into the secret, winter wonderland, while the rest of the world, it seemed, was fast asleep, deep in Christmas dreamland!

That, of course, may have been the case in the Upper World, but down below, in *Aqua Crysta*, sleep was the last thing on the troubled minds of the Aqua Crystans. Whether they were sat at tables in Galdo's market-place drinking fizzy bramble wine, or carving delicate crystal ornaments in the snug homesteads of Pillo, everyone was considering the words of Tregarth. They didn't *want* to believe him, but what he said definitely made some sort of sense...though only just! How could Queen Venetia be accused of treason? She had reigned for over forty glorious harvests. She was liked and trusted, and had held her office with pride. How *could* she be possibly guilty of betraying her people?

And what of her popular and respected advisor, Lepho? He, too, surely couldn't be accused of treachery! After all, it was Lepho who had saved the kingdom during the last harvest when soldiers from

the Upper World were threatening to destroy the *Harvestlands* and *Aqua Crysta* itself! No, he wouldn't do anything to harm the secret realm! Tregarth had even accused Jonathan and Jane, the last Upper World folk to come and live in *Aqua Crysta*, of being involved in the betrayal...but they had loved their little house in Pillo for the last fifty harvests. Surely nothing would drive them to harm their homeland!

And lastly, and even more incredibly, he had accused Jessica and Jamie of treason, the recent visitors from the Upper World - the ones who had helped *The Palace of Dancing Horses* come to life - the ones who had been called the 'saviours of *Aqua Crysta*', magically led to the secret kingdom in the first place!

Tregarth, however, was convinced that all six were guilty, and what's more, the Court he was about to set up would prove each and every charge of treason. Of this he had no doubt, and it was his address to those gathered in the *Meeting Hall Cavern* that would persuade all Aqua Crystans that he was right.

As the tall, broad shouldered, raven haired orator stood in the centre of the vast crystal studded cavern, his words held his audience spellbound. He held his listeners in the palm of his hand, especially when he kept repeating the phrases, *'the proof is all around you!'* and *'just feel it for yourselves!'*. The words echoed around the huge amphitheatre, each one accompanied by Tregarth's gloved fist rapping the crystal *Speaker's Lectern* before him.

But all this was beyond the ears of Jessica and Jamie. Their hearts wildly raced as they stepped into the snowy silence. Not a sound could be heard except for the gentle pitter patter of giant snow flakes as they added to the white, downy carpet which covered *Deer Leap's* back garden, and the sound of sinking wellington boots compacting the fresh snow.

Jessica, her long copper hair flowing from her scarlet bob cap and over the shoulders of her green waterproof, lead the way as they headed through the deep snow into the forest behind the cottage.

Jamie, following behind in his sister's footprints, shone his torch into the trees, his freckled face beaming under his mop of ginger hair.

The torch beam lit the never ending cascade of snowflakes as they fell to the forest floor or were captured by the ever thickening, white branches of the spruce trees.

Heavier and heavier the snow fell.

In no time, Jessica's bob cap was white. Even under the trees the snowflakes were so dense that the children felt almost breathless, as they plodded on, snowflakes constantly sticking to their faces before melting away.

"We'll be snowmen soon if we stay out here!" gasped Jessica, snowflakes pouring into her mouth.

Jamie overtook his sister and ran along one of the straight, narrow avenues between the ranks of spruce trees. Normally the avenues were carpeted with soft pine needles, but already they had been covered with this brand new, glistening blanket of snow.

George had been undisturbed while the children had lived at *Deer Leap*, although they knew that, one day, great swathes of trees would be felled. That's what their father was here to do. It had happened to the *Queen Mary* Forest in Scotland. Jessica and Jamie had loved her, but eventually she had had to go, and that's when their father had been appointed as Forest Manager of this forest on the Yorkshire Moors. One day the orders would be given and the great machines would be sent in to harvest the trees. That was why it had been planted in the first place, back in the 1950s. The trees were just like any other crop, but it took them tens of years to reach felling size. But, for the moment, *George* was a wonderful playground, full of hidden, secret places to be explored!

It wasn't long before Jamie reached the first small clearing which they'd discovered back in the autumn. Here in a perfect circle which they had named *The Dell* lay a couple of boulders they used as seats when they'd brought weekend picnics. Normally there was a soft carpet of pine needles and thick cushions of green moss on the boulders, but now all was pure white, beneath a wide column of tumbling snowflakes. It all looked just as inviting as it had been in autumn, even with the boulders each capped with snow and standing in the round, snowy patch like a pair of dwarf snowmen!

"Why don't we pile snow on top of the boulders to make a couple of snow giants?" laughed Jamie.

In next to no time, the two of them had buried the rocks and completely churned up the smooth plate of snow. Jessica added fallen twigs as arms and Jamie began to roll a great snowball as one of the heads.

And all the time, the snow continued to fall, on and on, the flakes becoming larger and larger. Jessica paused for a rest and looked up into the soft, feathery cascade. It almost made her gasp for breath as the huge flakes settled on her face and then melted.

"I know it sounds silly," she gasped, wiping the cold water from her nose and mouth, "but I'm absolutely boiling!"

"So am I!" panted Jamie, as he attempted to lift his giant snowball. "It must be because of all the hard work we're doing!"

"I think we ought to be getting back to *Deer Leap*," suggested Jessica. "We can come back and finish *Bill and Ben* after breakfast!"

"You know perfectly well that you won't want to come back today," replied Jamie. "It's Christmas Day remember? Once you've opened your presents nothing will drag you away from the cottage!"

It was at that moment that they both noticed something very peculiar happening beneath their feet. They both stared in astonishment as they saw patches of brown pine needles appearing amid the snow!

Each patch was growing and glistening with thousands of droplets of water.

"The snow's melting!" exclaimed Jamie, as he knelt and touched the forest floor beneath his feet. "And the ground feels warm!!"

As the two children stared in disbelief, the patches grew in size before their eyes. Patches merged with other patches and soon the whole round dell was brown instead of white, revealing its familiar cones, scattered twigs and tufts of pale green grass!

But still, the thick cascade of snowflakes continued to fall above it, each flake melting to nothing as it lightly touched the ground.

Jamie shone his torch into the forest. Beneath the trees, snow lay thick and smooth. He guided the beam round like a searchlight, illuminating the wide trunks and the heavily snow laden branches beyond the dell. But as the beam fell upon its far side it lit up a corridor of snowless forest floor stretching into the distance between two lines of trees!

Then the air became warmer and warmer, so much so that the tumbling snowflakes even vanished inches above the ground!

It was an amazing sight!

Jessica sank to the forest floor and unzipped her green waterproof and pulled off her scarlet bobcap.

"Phew!" she gasped as she wiped the moisture from her forehead and then pointed at the two snow giants. Before their eyes, like melting butter in a hot frying pan, each white giant began to shrink, revealing more and more of the two boulders. Water poured down their rough, rocky sides and seeped away beneath the pine needles. Soon, all that remained of *Bill and Ben* were two small mounds of snow perched on each boulder...and soon those, too, disappeared leaving just the two familiar cushions of soggy moss!

What had been, a few minutes earlier, a magical, wintery playground, had become, even more magically, the autumn forest dell!

Yet winter still surrounded it, except for the narrow, brown corridor, and winter still hung above it as the snow fell incessantly! If it had not been for the mysterious thaw, the snow would by now have been as deep as the boulders were high!

As the children gazed at the spectacular sight of this summer island in a winter's sea, they noticed a fine mist beginning to swirl and lap around the two silvery wet boulders.

"Can you smell anything?" asked Jessica, sniffing the air.

Jamie sniffed.

"Yes, I can...it's kind of...sweet!"

"Like the scent of the nutshell fires at Pillo...and the scent that drifted through the fallen ruins of the old barn where we found the crushed tricycle!" said Jessica.

"But we're nowhere near *Aqua Crysta!*" pointed out Jamie. "The Floss Cavern must be at least an hour away across the forest, following the old walls to the well!"

"Then there must be cracks and tunnels in the rocks leading from the cavern which have carried the warm air and scent from *Aqua Crysta!*" said Jessica.

"But we've been coming here most weekends since September and we've never noticed the warmth and the scent," said Jamie, mopping his glistening brow with the back of his mittens.

Then Jamie suddenly noticed his sister's face.

She seemed not to be listening and gazing into the distance behind him.

"What's up, Jess, what's the matter?"

Soundlessly, Jessica raised her right arm and pointed over Jamie's shoulder, not changing the stunned and shocked expression on her face.

Jamie slowly turned, and saw...standing as still as a statue...on the very edge of their secret dell....

Chapter 2

"And so...!" thundered Tregarth, his voice booming around the *Meeting Hall Cavern*. "...In conclusion!...I say to you *all*!...Every loyal citizen of *Aqua Crysta*!...We must act *now*!! We must put the Kingdom *first*!! We must act against all those who have *betrayed our precious realm*!!"

Tregarth paused, beads of sweat shining on his forehead, a steely determination beaming from his eyes, mesmerising his audience.

Then he took a step forward from the lectern and raised a single, menacing, gloved index finger. He pointed it at the silent, awe-struck Aqua Crystans like a threatening sword. Slowly, he moved it from side to side, its hypnotic power entrancing the hundreds of pairs of innocent, staring eyes. Then he dropped his voice almost to a whisper, his final words forced from behind clenched teeth...hissing, sizzling and spitting around the cavern.

"Sssave *Aqua Crysssta* now!...Sssoon it will be too late!...And you...will be the onesss that sssuffer!"

Again he paused, glaring at his flock. The sheep were in the pen. They were his. Four more words would complete the task.

"LONG LIVE *AQUA CRYSTA*!!" he suddenly roared, almost shaking the plunging stalactites from the cavern's roof.

"LONG LIVE *AQUA CRYSTA*!!" the flock sang out as one.

"LONG LIVE *AQUA CRYSTA*!!"

The gate of the pen slammed shut.

Tregarth was but a few steps from becoming King!

It had appeared soundlessly, like a phantom in the snowflakes.

It stood silently and unmoving like it was made of stone.

A roe deer - a young stag.

Still, so still, the deer remained, until suddenly, one of his fore-legs pawed the forest floor and his horned head bowed.

It was then that the children noticed a flash of colour around his neck...a flash of colour that instantly took their minds back to the magical realm of *Aqua Crysta* and especially to the crystal palace of its Queen. They both vividly remembered, as though it were yesterday, entering her sparkling rooms with the huge, magnificent jay feathers rising from the floors and curling along the ceilings. Jay feathers, the symbols of good fortune and prized by all Aqua Crystans, and now here, dozens of them entwined as a garland around the deer's slender neck. The iridescent greens and blues danced against the stag's chestnut fur, as slowly and gracefully, and not at all nervously, the regal animal stepped into the clearing.

Serenely, the fearless deer stepped onwards between the two boulders and towards the entranced children. His gleaming necklace seemed to shimmer more and more as if it had a life of its own. It was as though it was speaking for the deer, almost beckoning the children in some kind of mystical, silent language.

"This *has* to be something to do with *Aqua Crysta*" whispered Jessica, as the deer paused and bowed his head again, as though somehow greeting his onlookers. Pictures of *Chandar*, the albino fawn they had met in the late summer, flashed through both children's minds. She, too, had worn a jay feather necklace.

By now, although the snow continued to fall, the air above the clearing had become so warm that the tumbling flakes melted well above the small, velvety stubs on the deer's head that were the beginnings of immature antlers.

The sweet smelling mists thickened and swirled just above the ground almost erasing it from view. The clear, narrow corridor which stretched into the forest behind them also was awash with the warm, fragrant mist.

Carefully, so as not to alarm the deer, Jessica slowly got to her feet and gently put her hand out towards the deer's twitching nose.

Then, as Jessica looked at the two short, stubby, soft horns that sprouted from the brown fur between the stag's ears, she noticed something that made her gasp and spring backwards, almost startling the animal.

At the base of each young antler, where they emerged from the fur, like tree-saplings from autumn bracken, was....a tiny, tiny figure...each wrapped in a thick, heather coloured, hooded cloak and each bound to its horn by strands of plaited grass tied tightly round and round. Their heads had fallen forward, hidden by the cloaks' loose, baggy hoods.

Both figures were motionless and appeared unconscious...or worse! They were just drooping and probably would have collapsed had it not been for their plaited bonds.

"They're Aqua Crystans!" gasped Jamie. "We must rescue them...they could have been tied there for days, or weeks!"

"But who could have done such a thing?" wondered Jessica. "Why?"

The deer nudged Jessica's hand as she stroked his nose and then his forehead, gradually creeping her fingertips up to the tethered figures. Then the animal froze like a statue. He didn't move an inch, even when Jessica touched one of the cloaked shapes and then the other.

Each figure was no taller than a matchstick.

Both remained as still as stone, and Jessica began to think that they had fallen prey to the winter's night.

But suddenly, the drooping heads slowly began to stir.

"Look, look! They're moving! They're alive!" she called, making the stag's huge ears twitch for a moment. "Quickly, we've got to untie them! They must be freezing to death!"

"But how can we untie them?" asked Jamie. "The strands are so thin and close together!"

The two tiny hoods moved again and slowly lifted.

Meanwhile, the deer remained perfectly still, sensing that his tiny passengers had at last been found.

Then, as the heads lifted further, the hoods began to fall back and two ghostly white faces appeared with closed eyes...each face no larger than the nail of Jamie's little finger.

Jessica moved her face closer and closer to those of the two pitiful, bound figures...and then gasped again in amazement!!

She could hardly believe her eyes!

They were *Jonathan and Jane*!! The young brother and sister who they had met in *Aqua Crysta*...the two who had hosted the welcome party at their home in Pillo, and become their best friends! It seemed like only yesterday that Jessica and Jamie had met them on a crystal terrace way above Pillo with that wonderful view of the Pillo Falls at the end of the cavern! Only yesterday since their heroic adventures to save *Aqua Crysta* from the monstrous Upper World machines! Only yesterday since their farewells had echoed up and down the well as the pairs of children had parted before returning to their own worlds!

But now, in the depths of the Upper World winter, here were Jonathan and Jane, barely alive, tethered to the antlers of a roaming deer!

Jonathan was the first to open his eyes. They flickered open under his tousled mop of dark brown hair.

"Wh..where am I?" he mumbled as though stirring from a deep sleep. He raised his baggy sleeved arms and swept back his hood. He rubbed his eyes and then squinted as he looked at the two enormous faces before him.

15

An understandable look of horror suddenly crossed his face, but then he smiled.

"Jessica! Jamie!" he called in a tiny, slightly croaky voice. "At last, we've found you!"

Jane's eyes opened, and she too, beamed, reminding Jessica and Jamie of the smiling happy face framed by brown pig-tails they'd known back in the late summer during their first magical adventures. It was so sad to see them both looking so haggard and drawn, as though they had suffered great pain.

"We don't understand," whispered Jamie. "We thought you'd be snug and warm in Pillo, way beneath this wintery weather!"

Jonathan delved a hand into one of his deep cloak pockets and produced one of the familiar ruby-studded daggers. He began to cut the plaited strands that bound him so tightly to the deer horn.

"We'll explain as soon as we free ourselves," he gasped as he cut the tethers.

Soon, he had cut through all his bonds and tumbled forward onto the soft carpet of the deer's forehead. Quickly, he scrambled to his feet and freed his sister, who, when her tethers were severed, hugged her brother with a mixture of happiness and relief.

Then her tiny voice pierced the warm, still air, as she, amazingly shouted an order to the patient deer.

"Lie down, *Strike*!" she called. "Lie down!"

Both Jonathan and Jane clung tightly to the deer's horns as the young stag shuffled his feet, sank to his knees and then to the forest floor where he lay his head on a cushion of damp pine needles.

His passengers quickly, if a little unsteadily, trotted down between his huge, brown eyes, down his nose and jumped off onto the warm pine needles.

Jessica knelt down in the mists and invited her two friends to clamber up onto her palm. Before she could utter a word of welcome, Jonathan pleaded for both Jessica and Jamie to listen.

"Please, Jessica and Jamie," he started anxiously, "please will you help our Queen once again?"

Jane continued.

"We are in desperate trouble and a tragedy even worse than last time faces *Aqua Crysta* and her people!"

"If you come with us," burst Jonathan, "we will make sure that you return in next to no time, as you did before!"

Jamie well remembered his watch stopping at two minutes past two, and time standing still in *Aqua Crysta*, so both he and his sister didn't have to think twice about the request for help...despite knowing that it was Christmas morning and their father would be waking in a few hours time to his favourite day of the year! They just *had* to help! After all, it was only just after midnight! They were bound to be back home in time! Yes, they certainly had to help, whatever the crisis!

"But how can we possibly get to the well?" asked Jessica. "It'll take ages through all the snow!"

"No need to worry!" said Jane. "We'll take *Strike*!"

Jessica and Jamie looked at one another, both puzzled by Jane's suggestion, as though the deer was a Number 7 bus!

"It'll be OK!" laughed Jonathan. "He's brilliant and fast and knows the way through the forest to the well like the back of his..."

"Hoof, I suppose!" joked Jamie, beginning to be amazed by everything that was happening, but most of all, beginning to bubble with excitement at the thought of returning once again to the wonderful world of *Aqua Crysta*!

Less than a couple of minutes later, after tucking Jonathan and Jane snugly into their pyjama pockets, Strike was leaping through *George's* deepest depths, following the snowless corridor, with Jessica and Jamie clinging on as tightly as they could. It felt almost as if they were flying through the trees as the young deer glided along the avenues of spruce and larch.

Sometimes they could feel the warmth of the air and smell the sweet, nutty aroma from the rocks below as Strike sprinted over stretches of the brown, pine-needle covered forest floor where the snow had melted.

At other times the stag leapt over gentle drifts of snow and disturbed heavily laden white branches, making Jessica and

Jamie gasp for breath as fallen snow swished around their faces. Behind them, Strike left a light thread of footprints sewn neatly between the trees, and every now and again, the nimble deer sprang over the familiar low stone walls that criss-crossed the forest - the stone walls that had led the children into their unbelievable adventures in the first place!

Soon, he was climbing Old Soulsyke Farm's gentle hill. Here, the snow was at its deepest with the huge, tall, leafless trees being far apart compared to the closely packed pine trees of the rest of the forest. Strike slowed as he climbed the slope and then suddenly the wonderful view of the old ruined farm met the children's squinted eyes. Old Soulsyke looked like a beautiful Christmas cake, absolutely covered in thick snow. Memories of their first visit, back in August, filled the children's minds...discovering "J and J's" map, *Spook*, the white cat, not to mention the place turning into a fortress with all that barbed wire and the look-out towers!

Strike raised his paws high as he made his way past the farm through the deep snow. The sudden change of speed gave Jessica and Jamie a chance to check on their own passengers. They were fine and although not perfectly comfortable in the pyjama pockets, it was certainly a big improvement on their last journey!
All the time, Jessica and Jamie thought about the problem that had forced Jonathan and Jane to find them in the first place. Was it something to do with the warmth they had felt back at *The Dell*? Whatever it was, they hadn't a clue how they could be of any help, but they were determined to find out...as long as they were back for Christmas Day!

Soon, they had left the farm behind and once again Strike began to canter lightly over the snow, although gradually more and more stretches of bare forest floor could be seen amid wedges of white. And by the time they approached the gateposts near the well, snow was completely absent beneath the trees although snowflakes were still falling into the dripping treetops above. The children knew that the

Floss Cavern was directly below, and their hearts began to beat faster as they thought about what lay ahead...or rather, *below*!

The young stag smoothly came to a halt and Jessica and Jamie were back at the exact spot where they had slept beneath the stars. The exact spot where they'd been woken in the deep darkness of the night by the rustling deer and then plucked up the courage to descend into the wide open mouth of the well.

Strike pawed the forest floor as if to say farewell and the two children dismounted. Jamie stroked his head and knowing the value of the wonderful jay feather garland to the people of *Aqua Crysta*, slipped the colourful necklace from the stag and placed it over his sister's head to settle on her shoulders.

"A gift for Queen Venetia when we meet her again!" he said, and, almost at once, Jessica's slightly growing anxiety was relieved.

"I can hardly wait to get down there!" she said excitedly, looking around for the hidden well-head stone slabs.

As they both began to scrape away the thin grassy cover they turned to see if Strike was still there.

But he'd vanished...disappeared into the depths of the snowy forest, his job done.

All was quiet and still, with just the sound of dripping water. The children were alone...although not quite...as a tiny voice called from Jessica's pyjama pocket beneath her green waterproof.

"Your journey will be safe now that you are wearing the feather garland!" called Jane. "But please hurry so we can help the Queen!"

"You mean the Queen herself is in danger?" burst Jamie, at last getting a hint of what all the trouble was about.

"You'll find out soon enough!" called Jonathan from Jamie's pyjama pocket. "So, come on, let's get down the well!"

As they began to pull back the thin turf, revealing the rough, grimy slabs of stone, Jessica suddenly stopped.

"Something's just occurred to me!" she whispered, hoping Jonathan and Jane couldn't hear her.

"It's just occurred to me as well!" whispered back Jamie, as usual thinking the same thoughts as his sister. "The rope you mean?"

He stopped just as he was about to heave up one of the slabs to open the deep well.

"We can't just jump off the last rung into *Aqua Crysta* - we'll have no way of climbing back up!" whispered Jessica.

Indeed, the rope was neatly curled on the floor of *Deer Leap's* garden shed. Jamie had recovered it at the end of their last adventure and taken it home. Without the rope they would be stranded in *Aqua Crysta* with no way back...not only to Christmas Day...but to their Upper World full size!

But how were they going to tell Jonathan and Jane?

How could they tell them that their hazardous quest had all been in vain...and that after all they had been through in trying to find them, they couldn't go with them back to *Aqua Crysta*??

Chapter 3

Jessica and Jamie gloomily sat back against a drift of moist pine-needles, downcast by the thoughts that had sapped away their expectations. Moments before, they had been enrapt with the images of *Aqua Crysta* that had lingered with them since late summer. Now, as they sat, considering what to do, the warm, scented air rising from the magical realm beneath almost urged them to open the well-head as if it had a power all of its own!

"But, what's the point of opening the well? We can't go down!" said Jessica glumly, as her brother began to finger the edge of one of the stone slabs. Unable to resist, Jessica's fingers, too, began to grip the same rough stone.

"After *three*!" called Jamie.

They each tightly gripped an opposite edge of the slab.

"One...two...*three*!!"

They lifted together, and the stone slab rose and fell backwards onto the forest floor with a thud, just as it had done at the end of August.

A gush of warm, sweet air swirled around their faces like the last time...as though the well was breathing out, gasping with relief after having been blocked since the late summer.

"Listen, Jess!" whispered Jamie, pointing down into the dark depths.
A sound they knew only too well came from the black depths.
The long, eerie tone of a single musical note from a horn filled the well
and spilled out into the ghostly forest.
"We've got to go now! They've heard us! They know we're here!" burst
Jamie.
"But...we can't!" resisted Jessica. "We'll never be able to re..!"
"Wait a sec! I've got it!" exclaimed Jamie, unzipping his waterproof and
pulling out his long, red scarf.
"Our scarves! If we knot them together and dangle them from the
ladder's last rung..."
"...We'll be able to return like last time!" finished Jessica excitedly,
overwhelmed by lure of the magic.
At that moment they were both startled by Jane's tiny voice.
"Please, please, hurry...the longer we take, the greater the danger for the
Queen!" she pleaded.

       Tregarth's trap had been well and truly sprung! There
was now no turning back. The bait had captured its prey. Jonathan and
Jane, curled up quietly in their pyjama pockets, both felt sadder and

more down-hearted than they had ever
felt in their lives. Would their Upper
World friends ever forgive them for
leading them into the grip of the
treacherous Tregarth? They kept their
thoughts to themselves, but their feelings
of guilt were hard to bear.

       With Jamie's torch
beam leading the way into the depths, the
two innocent, unwary captives sank into
Aqua Crysta's beguiling grasp...or, rather,
into the dangerous grasp of one of her
inhabitants!

Jessica and Jamie, completely unaware that they were falling into Tregarth's web, began the long climb down into the magical kingdom. Soon, they were level with the ledge that lead to the door to the wonderful forest cellar...*The Palace of Dancing Horses*, because of the gleaming carousel that was the centre-piece of the tin toy, clockwork fairground.

Both Jessica and Jamie would liked to have had a quick peep at the treasures beyond the door, but realised the urgency of their mission. They also realised that it was here where they would have to part company with Jonathan and Jane for a while. No Aqua Crystan could return to the Floss Cavern by way of the well as they would shrink into almost invisibility. Jonathan and Jane would have to return through the forest cellar and the Harvest Passageway.

Carefully, Jessica and Jamie removed their rather quiet and sad passengers from their pyjama pockets and placed them gently on the ledge which led to the wooden door. Jamie shone his torch on the gap beneath the door through which his tiny friends would walk easily into the Palace.

"But how are you going to find your way down the Harvest Passageway to *Aqua Crysta*?" asked Jessica, suddenly remembering the dark, rocky route and its dangers! She would never ever forget the encounter with the giant mouse!

"Don't worry, Jess. All that has been taken care of," replied Jonathan gloomily. "Our friends will have left us a crystal or two to light our way. They should be just beyond the door."

Jessica had noticed the sombre mood which had swept over both Jonathan and his sister.

"If you don't mind me saying, you seem a little...unhappy...worried. I thought you would be bursting to get back to...."

"We're both weary after our ordeal in the Upper World," gasped Jane, trying to disguise her guilt. She knew what lay ahead, but just could not give anything away or it could put in peril the whole mission.

"We'll see you down in *Aqua Crysta* then!" beamed Jonathan uncomfortably, also torn by guilty feelings.

And with that, the tiny Aqua Crystans turned and headed towards the gap beneath the wooden door, waving as they went.

"Good luck!" called Jamie. "We'll see you soon and then you can tell us why you were tied to Strike's horns!"

With a last wave, Jonathan and Jane disappeared under the door and were gone, leaving Jessica and Jamie alone between worlds and with strange feelings about what lay ahead.

"They seemed so sad, didn't they?" sighed Jessica. "As though they wanted to tell us *something* and couldn't bring themselves to say *anything*!"

As they gripped the metal ladder rungs tightly, the warm, scented air from below swirled around them, like magic fingers enticing them to descend further and removing any doubts about the task ahead.

Soon, below their feet, they could just about make out the milky disc in the distance which they now knew to be the glow of the Crystal Cavern's rocks beyond the bottom of the well. Brighter and brighter it grew until there was no need at all for torchlight. A good job, too, as its battery was just about dead.

At last, Jamie reached the last rung and rested to wipe the sweat from his forehead.

"It certainly is a lot warmer than last time!" he panted.

"You can say that again!" gasped Jessica.

"It certainly is a lot...!" laughed Jamie.

"OK, OK, clever clogs! Let's knot our scarves together!" said Jessica.

Although they didn't say much about the jump ahead, both children were inwardly nervous. Partly about the

suspicions aroused by the mood of Jonathan and Jane as they left, and partly about whether the jump would have the same safe landing as in the summer. Then, when they had jumped they didn't know they were going to shrink, but now, nervous thoughts flashed through their minds about suddenly shrinking from Upper World dimensions to Aqua Crystan dimensions where they would be about as tall as an Upper World little finger!

But still, the alluring kingdom beckoned them on, and soon they had threaded the knotted scarves through the last rung so that the chunky knot sat on the iron bar and the two scarves dangled into the cavern.

What only seemed to be a small leap away through wispy, swirling mist was the thin, shimmering trickle of water flowing amid pink and white glowing rocks. It looked no more than an inch or two wide, but they knew it to be a vast, wide torrent of frothy water wider than an Upper World motorway in a cavern as high as the clouds!

When all was ready, Jamie tucked his torch into his waterproof's pocket and then glanced up at his sister.

"See you in a couple of secs, Jess!"

"Good luck!" she replied. "I'll try not to land on top of you!"

Jamie then took a deep breath and plunged into the timeless, shrunken world of *Aqua Crysta*.

A moment later he crunched onto the pebbles on the shore of the River Floss. He just had time to gaze way up into the mist which hid the bottom of the well and his sister, when he felt grabbing fingers digging roughly into his shoulders. He instantly turned and saw a hooded face staring at him with angry, furrowed eyebrows and a grim, iron mouth. He'd never seen such a fearsome face in his life!

"Jessica!!" he shouted at the top of his voice. *"JESSICA!! DON'T JUM..!!"*

But his warning was cut short by a rough, steely hand closing over his mouth, gripping his jaw like a vice. He struggled, but the more he did, the tighter the vice gripped, until he thought his jaw was going to be put out of joint.

He stared helplessly skywards as his sister's enormous wellington boots' zig-zag soles thrust themselves through the mist. He blinked, and the next moment Jessica crunched onto the river shore and was grabbed by another hostile, hooded Aqua Crystan! Others stood in a menacing group glaring at their captives, each of them displaying anything but welcome on their faces. Gone were the beaming, smiling, carefree folk that Jessica and Jamie remembered from their summer visit. Their hearts sank.

Struggling was useless against such hostility and strength so both children stopped and instead became rigid with fear, especially when the tallest of their captors suddenly spoke with a deep, grave voice.

"We make no apologies for your treatment," he began, "and what is more, we hold you personally responsible for the ills that have befallen *Aqua Crysta* since you first came! The Queen is blind to your guilt, and we hope that by capturing you and holding you hostage, we will change her mind!"

Behind the bars of rough fingers which smothered their faces, Jessica and Jamie were more frightened than at anytime in their lives. Instead of the warmth and friendliness they had known on their last visit, they had, this time, fallen into the depths of a nightmare. Thoughts of being trapped in it forever and never returning to snug *Deer Leap* cottage, their father and Christmas Day made them both inwardly panic, although they knew they had to remain calm.

Jessica began to feel breathless and stifled by the grip of her captor. Both children were by now becoming hotter and hotter. Their faces

27

glistened with sweat...as did the stern faces beneath their hoods.
It seemed hotter than the hottest of summer days.
They could hardly believe it. Only a short while ago they had been looking out of *Deer Leap's* window upon a snowy, wintery scene, but now they were sweltering in the heat of a raging furnace made worse by the sticky, damp, humid swirling mists above the Floss.

Jessica just had to break free, otherwise she feared she would faint. She desperately tugged at the unmoving fingers that were clamped over her mouth. Her heart raced. She began to feel dizzy. Everything around her began to swim and swirl!
Consciousness was slipping away...
she fought...to hang on...but...
...she was powerless...to resist...
...her eyes closed...and she knew no more...!

Suddenly, her eyes sprung open...or at least she thought they'd sprung open! Her fingers touched her eye lids to make sure. Yes, they were open...but she couldn't see anything but blackness. Solid, impenetrable blackness!
It wasn't her bedroom at *Deer Leap* for certain! Even on the darkest of nights she could always make out her curtains and the end of her wardrobe. But they had gone...and it was so warm and sticky...and there was the never ending din of torrenting water...and instead of soft sheets and her cosy duvet, there was rough, gritty rock and sharp stones grating her fingertips!
She sat up and heard the crinkle of her waterproof and sensed that she was wearing her wellington boots! She moved her arms in front of her like the feelers of a butterfly and felt nothing but warm air, except behind where she felt the blackness become solid in the form of a wall of rock.
"You've come round at last!" came a familiar whisper in the dark.
"Where am I? What's happened?" whispered Jessica.
"We've been captured and thrown in a cell," said Jamie, fiddling with

his lifeless torch. "I can't see a thing. It's been terrible just lying here waiting for you to wake up. You fainted on the river shore."

"But how did we get here?" mumbled Jessica, still a bit groggy and dazed.

"We jumped into *Aqua Crysta*, remember?" said Jamie. "Then we were grabbed by a gang of pretty nasty, angry, ugly Aqua Crystans who marched me here and carried you! We're in this black cellar somewhere near the foot of the stairway that leads up to the *Larder Caves*. We're by the Floss. That's what that racket is outside!"

As Jessica's eyes gradually got used to the gloom, she began to make out a few glowing crystals embedded in the prison walls and then a faint strip of light coming from beneath what she presumed must be a door. Then she made out the dim outline of her brother who was sitting by the wall a couple of feet away. She reached out to touch him to make sure he was really there.

Jamie suddenly screamed out,

"What's that? There's fingers on my cheek!"

"It's only me, silly! I can't see you properly!"

"Sshh! What's that?" gasped Jamie.

"What's what?" whispered Jessica, goosebumps rising on the back of her neck.

"Th..that!" gasped Jamie with a cold shiver.

A sound...a groan...was coming from the rocky cell's deep, spooky blackness.

The children were not alone.

Some*one*...or some*thing*...

...was there!!

Chapter 4

"There it is again!" whispered Jamie, stumbling forward onto
his knees.

A second groan, louder than the first, rumbled from somewhere in the
pitch blackness.

"It sounds like someone in pain!" gasped Jessica, slowly standing up.

They both froze, with just their heartbeats ringing in their ears.

Inch by inch, Jessica shuffled forwards over the gritty floor, fearful that
she might suddenly plunge into a deep, invisible hole.

Then a third groan, even louder, filled their ears.

"Who's there?" called Jamie softly. "Where are you?"

"O..ver...he..re!" came a weak, pained voice.

Jessica inched forward towards the sound, followed by her brother.

"Where are you?" she mumbled.

"I...I know...that voice," replied the darkness. "It's *Jessica*!...from the
Upper World!...isn't it?"

"*Lepho*!" burst Jamie. "It's *Lepho*!"

Jessica suddenly tripped and fell onto welcome softness...

"You've found me, alright!" Lepho painfully laughed, warming the
hearts of the two children. At last, the friendliness they had expected to
find in *Aqua Crysta*!

Lepho had guided and befriended them on their last visit. He was the Queen's valuable advisor and companion.

"You don't sound well at all!" said Jamie.

"It's just my head. I've just been questioned again by Tregarth's side-kicks. When they'd finished with me, they threw me back into the dark. I seem to have been locked in here for half a lifetime!"

"Tregarth? Who's *Tregarth*?" asked Jessica.

"It's a long story," replied Lepho, "but first I must say how good it is to see, or rather hear you again! Although I wish the circumstances of our meeting were more pleasant! Tregarth's scheming plan has obviously worked well...very well, indeed!"

"Plan? What are you talking about?" Jamie asked, even more puzzled.

"I know it must seem to you that I am speaking in riddles and the story I have to tell will sadden you..."

"But please tell us, if you have the strength!" pleaded Jessica.

Lepho raised himself into a sitting position in the darkness and cleared his throat.

"It all began after the last harvest expedition had returned from the forest with its gatherings of berries and nuts and all. It was at a time that was between autumn and the onset of winter in your Upper World...a time we call *'Wintumn'*."

Unbeknown to one another, Jessica and Jamie both smiled at the word and began to feel happier. It was amazing the effect of Lepho's voice. They somehow felt relaxed and comfortable with him, as they had been on their summer visit. A chink of hope to match the chink of light from beneath the door.

Lepho continued.

"The first frosts had crisped the fallen leaves and there had even been an early sprinkle of snow. Queen Venetia had proclaimed, as was the tradition, that there should be no more journeys to the Upper World until the Sun warmed your lands again. It was then that the troubles began..."

31

"But I can't imagine any kind of trouble in your world of peace and harmony!" said a puzzled Jamie.

"It is true, our world has known peace and harmony for centuries upon centuries...until now!" continued Lepho, his tone becoming solemn.

"The Queen is desperately sad, especially after the wonders you performed with Jonathan and Jane in bringing life into the *Palace of Dancing Horses*. Every citizen of *Aqua Crysta* was delighted by your endeavours...but, now..."

Lepho paused.

"Now what?" asked Jessica, again suddenly anxious about what could follow.

"But, now..." Lepho went on, thankful in a way for the dark, "your names are despised and hated!!"

"But why?" burst Jessica at once feeling the weight of all the rocks above her on her heart. "What have we done wrong?"

"Nothing, nothing at all" admitted Lepho, "and that is the view of the Queen and those who advise her, especially Mayor Merrick!"

"But I still don't see what we've done to make everyone so angry!" said Jamie, beginning to feel frustrated and annoyed.

"You have done nothing, but Tregarth has stirred up the myth that you have brought ill fortune upon *Aqua Crysta*. Jonathan and Jane have been cast in the same evil role together with myself and the Queen. All six of us have been accused of *treason*!"

Jessica and Jamie just couldn't believe what they were hearing! 'Treason' was a word they associated with medieval kings and the Tower of London, heads being chopped off and Guy Fawkes!

"Tregarth even set up a court in Pillo's market place and treason was its verdict!"

"But how can we be traitors...we *helped* you all back in the summer?"

Lepho paused and then he told of how the River Floss had brought trouble and strife to all the inhabitants of Galdo and Pillo. Its flow had become unsteady and unpredictable. Floods had washed away market stalls and even people's belongings from their houses. There had been times of drought when the giant cascades at each end of the Floss Cavern had failed to churn up the usual amounts of froth. And, as it was believed that it was the river's froth which produced the magical mists that prolonged life and stopped time and decay in *Aqua Crysta*, then its sudden absence was taken seriously...very seriously, indeed!

Then, to add grief upon grief, the water, and with it, the air of *Aqua Crysta* had become hotter and hotter and hotter, causing even more dismay...and anger...among the Queen's people.

Tregarth had become the figurehead, the spokesman for the growing discontent, which then lead to protests and even rebellion. He convinced the masses who listened to his speeches that the blame lay fairly and squarely at the feet of those who had been involved with the goings on in the Upper World at the end of the summer.

Lepho came to the end of his sad tale,

"The court, with Tregarth as Chief Judge and a baying crowd as jury, decided that I should be imprisoned and that Jonathan and Jane should be sent to trick you two into returning to *Aqua Crysta* to become hostages to force Queen Venetia into admitting her part in the woeful events...and forcing her to leave the throne..."

"So Tregarth can seize the throne and become King himself, no doubt!!" gasped Jessica in disbelief.

Jessica and Jamie had listened with more and more amazement as Lepho had unravelled his tragic story and how they had become entangled within it. They now understood why Jonathan and Jane had seemed so uncomfortable and uneasy with what they were doing...as though they held a grave secret they could not tell.

In the silence that followed in the rocky blackness they found it hard to believe that during the last happy two or three weeks of the school term, during those joyful rehearsals for the Christmas Concert...during the happiness and laughter of putting up the decorations and the Christmas tree with their father at *Deer Leap*...during all that time...unknown to them...they had been tried by a court, their names had become hated and trampled, and their capture had been plotted!!

Shivers went up and down their spines as they wondered what was now going to happen to them...and when!

"Jonathan and Jane were put into a terrible position!" said Jamie, at last.

"They had no choice," sighed Lepho. "They dared not say anything to you of the real reasons for their plea for you to return to *Aqua Crysta*. Once the trial was over, Tregarth summoned his most obedient deer of the forest, the young stag, Strike, and your two friends were bound to his horns and he was commanded to roam the forest until he encountered yourselves. The crazed venture could have easily ended in the deaths of Jonathan and Jane with the harshness of winter...but, that is, and always will be, the nature of the scheming, evil Tregarth!"

"If it hadn't been for us creeping downstairs to put dad's presents under the tree...and then me seeing the snow falling...we would never have seen Strike!" said Jamie.

"And another day and night of ice and snow would surely have killed Jonathan and Jane!" said Jessica angrily.

"And what's this power that Tregarth has?" asked Jamie. "How can a man no larger than my little finger command a wild animal?"

"It is magic which Tregarth and his ancestors have possessed for as long as there have been people living in *Aqua Crysta*...but it has never been used for evil..."

"Until now!" snapped Jessica.

"All this explains *George's* mysterious melting snow!" said Jamie, "and the snowflakes that didn't reach the ground...it was the heat rising from..."

Suddenly, the cell door flew open and the three prisoners were bathed in bright light, so much so that they had to cover their eyes from the sudden glare. Jessica and Jamie squinted through their fingers.

In the dazzling doorway, with shadows almost reaching the cowering captives, were three figures. Two small ones at either side of a third giant middle one!

Just like salt and pepper and the vinegar bottle on *Deer Leap's* kitchen table!

"Jonathan and Jane," whispered Lepho.

"Who's the other?" asked Jessica in her quietest whisper.

"That's Tregarth!" replied Lepho with a tremor in his usually calm, confident voice. "*Tregarth the Terrible!*"

Chapter 5

"Jonathan! Jane!" called Jessica with welcoming outstretched arms. The two small figures framed in the bright doorway ran across the cellar floor and hugged the two victims of Tregarth's trickery. They had been uncertain of what Jessica and Jamies' reaction would be when they eventually met. Thankfully they seemed forgiven.

The giant figure of Tregarth took a step forward, casting his giant shadow over his five prisoners like a fishing net.

"Well, well, well!!" suddenly came the deep, powerful tones of Tregarth, rolling round the walls and filling every nook and cranny. "That makes all five caught in my web at last! Now we can do a little bargaining with the woman on the throne...with your co-operation, of course!!"

"And what if we do not offer you our *co-operation*, as you put it?" enquired Lepho, defiantly.

"You are far wiser than that, my friend!" replied Tregarth. "I am well aware of your ambition to become Mayor of Pillo after that bumbling fool, Merrick. You do business with me, and I will grant you that particular gold chain of office when I become King. All you have to do is to persuade Venetia to give up her ancestors' throne in favour of the people's choice...*my very self*!!"

"The people have had no say in the matter and you know it!" barked Lepho. "You know as well as I, that you have stirred up this hatred of myself and my friends here, just to further your own ambitions! You know we are not to blame for the ill-fortune that befalls our Land. You want the throne for yourself and stirring up this discontent is..."

"Treason! *You* are the traitor! You will *never* sit on the throne!" exclaimed Jonathan furiously and bravely. "We'll make sure you don't!"

"And how do you intend to do that, young man?"growled Tregarth angrily, stepping forward and raising his arm as if to strike Jonathan. Lepho quickly stopped him.

"You touch a hair of his head and you will answer to me!" bellowed Lepho, staring up at the giant who towered head and shoulders above him.

Tregarth withdrew and laughed deeply as he moved back towards the door and once again became a silhouette against the bright crystal light of the Cavern.

"I personally will inform Her Majesty of the news that all five treacherous enemies of the Realm are now locked away and can do no further harm!" he laughed, "and, what is more, that you, Lepho, will shortly plead with her to leave the throne!"

Lepho lunged forward, determined to teach Tregarth a lesson he would never forget, but suddenly the cellar was plunged back into darkness as the door slammed shut and the lock snapped fast.

Lepho shuffled back to the four children and slowly sat between the two pairs. All five could just about make out one another in the dribble of light from beneath the door.

No one said a word for a while, but eventually Jamie broke the silence by characteristically wondering whether or not it would be worthwhile trying to find another way out of the cellar. But, Lepho, much to Jamie's disappointment, said that he had known the *Understairs Cellar* for as long as he could remember and there was definitely no secret exit.

They were all well and truly entangled in Tregarth's web!

Silence once more fell upon the quintet, and, one by one, they lay down on the cellar's rocky floor and drifted into sleep.

It was Jessica's eyes that suddenly sprung open and gazed into the depths of darkness that surrounded her. Was she in her bedroom at *Deer Leap*? Was it time to get up? It was Christmas morning and there were presents to open! Would Dad like his socks? More importantly would he like the 1960s music album they'd found at a car-boot sale?

It was then that she realised she was not curled up in her bed, nor were there any signs of dawn creeping in through her bedroom curtains.

Her fingers instead felt the rough, stony floor and she sensed the other four sleeping nearby. Or, was this a Christmas Eve dream while she was still asleep?

It was difficult to tell in the pitch darkness, even with her eyes wide open!

But then she heard it!

The sound that had woken her!

A clicking sound from the door!

She heard it again!

She propped herself up on her elbow and gazed at the door.

She could just make out some kind of movement disturbing the thin bar of light in the gap at the foot of the door.

Then she heard the lock's bolt clatter.

The door began to move.

As it slowly opened another vertical band lit the four sleeping shapes in front of her.

Was it Tregarth returning for Lepho?

A silhouetted hooded figure appeared in the column of bright light.

No, it couldn't be Tregarth. This figure was nowhere near as large.

It was much slighter and shorter.

The figure swiftly entered the cellar and then gently, soundlessly, closed the door so that the light was once more blotted out.

The dark shape hovered like a black ghost. Unmoving and faceless, the eerie shape almost made Jessica want to scream out or bury her head in her hands.

Instead, she watched it intently, her heart beating faster and faster.

Then the figure began to shuffle forward, unsure in the dark.

Larger and larger it grew until it towered over Jessica and the knot of sleeping captives.

It was then that Jessica noticed in the gloom that the strange visitor was carrying before it what seemed to be a sort of tray! Surely not Tregarth's servant with a tray of refreshments?

Suddenly all hell broke loose in the deadly tomb!

The figure tripped over Jamie's sprawling legs and plunged headlong on top of Jonathan and Jane!

Instantly, the jumble of cloaks, wellington boots and waterproofs stirred. The tray and its contents flew everywhere as Lepho wrestled the stranger to the ground and swept back the hood to reveal the identity of the black ghost.

It was difficult to see in the gloom, but suddenly a terrified voice screamed out in the chaos.

"It's me...*Venetia*...your *Queen!*"

Lepho's face must have been a joy to behold if only they could have seen it!

At once, he released his grip and helped the dishevelled lady to her feet, uttering as many words of apology as he could muster!

On learning of the capture of her five noble and heroic friends, Queen Venetia had, in disguise, travelled alone down the Floss as a passenger on Captain Frumo's ship, the *Goldcrest*. She had disembarked at the Larder Stairway and quietly produced the tray and food which she had concealed beneath her cloak. Then, her face well hidden by her hood, she had made her way to the *Understairs Cellar* as a servant unquestioned by anyone.

Once there, she had simply unhooked the key and opened the door! "It's the last thing that the demon Tregarth would have expected!" laughed the Queen triumphantly. "I cannot just sit and wait for him to take the throne. We've got to fight back!"

It was at that moment the Queen produced another surprise. She seemed to reach beneath her cloak and revealed a pouch closed tightly at the neck by a draw-string. She opened it and out flooded the most wonderful light from a large crystal. Immediately, the cellar was awash with its beams illuminating every nook and cranny and the amazed faces of the five prisoners. They stared at the familiar

 beautiful face of the Queen, framed by its cascade of golden hair, and she in turn hugged her friends. She then plucked four more crystals from the soft pouch like eggs from a nest. Each shone brilliantly as she gave one to each of the captives.

The Cellar shone even more brightly as Jessica and Jamie saw clearly for the first time the faces of their companions. Lepho's ginger hair blazed suddenly into life like a miniature bonfire above his freckle dashed face, while the faces of dark haired Jonathan and Jane were lit at once by broad smiles. Lepho was dressed in his usual heathery cloak, Jonathan in his familiar, baggy green corduroy short trousers, checked shirt and striped sleeveless pullover, Jane in her flowery, lace-necked frock, pink ribboned pigtails and white socks. Sadly, they all looked pale and unwell after their ordeals, but their spirits seemed as determined and strong as ever.

Glistening tears flowed down the cheeks of the Queen like a trickle of tiny diamonds as she quickly gathered the slices of toasted acorns and toadstools she had brought on the tray.

"I shall never forgive the evil Tregarth for bonding you to Strike's horns and compelling you to wander helplessly in the winter wilderness at the mercy of the cold and ice!" she sobbed as she gave Jonathan and Jane the food. "Nor shall I forgive him the treatment he has forced upon you, Lepho, and you two, Jessica and Jamie. His trickery and treason, his cruel court and his turning of my people against your names will not go unpunished!"

For a while, the prisoners ate heartily and soon there wasn't a single crumb left.

"We must somehow show the people of *Aqua Crysta* that Tregarth is the evil, plotting rogue we know him to be!" said Lepho, at last.

"And make sure he never becomes King!" insisted Jane.

"But the question is, how?" asked Jonathan, solemnly.

Queen Venetia stood gracefully and then looked at her loyal friends one by one.

"I, too, have a plan!" she said in a voice full of determination.

"But before I tell you of it, please let me thank you for your support. The ordeals you have faced have been hard and cruel and for their endurance I thank you from the bottom of my heart. Once this is over, you will be well rewarded..."

"No reward will be necessary, Your Majesty!" said Jonathan, jumping to his feet and kissing the Queen's hand.

"You know that we will do anything to ensure that you remain Queen!" said Jessica echoed by Jamie.

"Tell us of your plan!" said Lepho, anxiously. "If you do not return to Galdo soon, Tregarth will seize the throne in your absence!"

"Fear not! When the river turns I shall be on Frumo's ship back to Galdo. I have made sure that Tregarth is well occupied in Pillo by false promises and tittle-tattle I dispatched with a loyal envoy. He will be considering my letter as we speak!"

The Queen paused and then continued.

"First, let me tell you of the *Crown of Rasinja,* which will prove once and for all to my people that the ill fortunes we have suffered in recent times is not of *your* making, but have been brought about by the crown itself!"

"But how can a mere crown possibly make the Floss flood, warm its waters and lose its mystic froth?" asked Lepho.

"The *Crown of Rasinja* is no mere crown!" said the Queen calmly. "It is a crown that has powers which were brought across the sea from a far-off Land many Upper World centuries ago, even before the great abbeys and churches of England were destroyed by the Tudor King Henry the Eighth. The Abbot of Whitby Abbey, when he fled from Henry's destroyers, nearly five centuries ago, entrusted the safe keeping of the Abbey's treasures to the faithful monk, Murgwyn. It was he who had discovered the well and the hidden cellar near Old Soulsyke Farm. Sadly, most of the treasures were lost or stolen on their way from the ravaged cliff-top abbey to Old Soulsyke, but the *Crown of Rasinja* reached the cellar safely. When Murgwyn discovered the magical powers of the Crystal Cavern which lay below the well, he and his followers became the first inhabitants of *Aqua Crysta*, and Murgwyn became the first King. All the remaining treasure shrunk with them on their journey into *Aqua Crysta* - all, that is, except the *Crown of Rasinja!*"

"Where's the crown now?" exclaimed Jessica, who always enjoyed an historical mystery.

"The *Crown of Rasinja*, because of its respected mystical powers, was later taken down the Harvest Passageway into *Aqua Crysta* still in its full Upper World size. Fortunately it was made originally of eight separate parts so that it could be easily hidden if its royal wearer was attacked. This meant that it could be taken down the Harvest Passageway in pieces. It was then decided by Murgwyn to hide the crown deep beneath the Crystal Cavern where it could be reassembled...but nobody now knows exactly of its location...because the Aqua Crystans who toiled with its great weight and size never returned! All we know is that it lies somewhere beyond the *Cave of Torrents*, where no Aqua Crystan has dared to venture ever since..."

"But why? What's so bad about the *Cave of Torrents*?" burst Jamie, equally liking a spooky mystery.

"More of that later, Jamie," Lepho interrupted. "Let Her Majesty finish her tale."

The Queen smiled at Jamie's enthusiasm and continued.

"As you know, because of the great age to which all Aqua Crystans live, I am only the fourth to have sat on the throne. Sigmund, my greatly missed husband, before me, then his father before him, who was the son of the first King Murgwyn."

She paused again, and then sat with her five listeners. She dropped her voice to a whisper. Everyone wondered what was coming next, even Lepho, who thought he knew all of *Aqua Crysta*'s secrets.

"The throne upon which we have all sat, itself holds one of the greatest secrets of our Realm. The throne was carved from elmwood and crystal by Murgwyn and it was he who concealed within its seat a box...a box which contains a parchment written by the last Abbot of Whitby Abbey. The words on this parchment have only

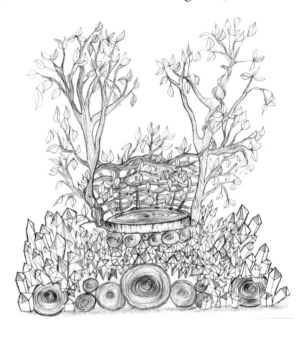

been known to the four monarchs of *Aqua Crysta*. Their eyes alone have seen the words... that is, until...*now*!"

Her small audience gazed in amazement as, once more, like a magician, the Queen delved into the soft pouch which had held the crystals, and withdrew a frail, rolled parchment tied with

43

curled, leafy twigs. Her green eyes sparkled in the crystal light as her long, slender fingers began to slowly undo the woody strands and unroll the ancient document.

Her face, framed with her long, golden hair, broke into a knowing smile, as if she knew that the words held the solution to all of *Aqua Crysta*'s ills.

With the five crystals clustered around her like a constellation of stars, she began to read the faded words...

Chapter 6

"In Depths So Deep
Beneath This Seat,
Even Beyond
Where Five Caves Meet,

Jewels And Gold
In Dark And Cold,
This Realm And Throne
For All Time Hold.

But If These Gems,
Should Hate Their Place,
Times Of Trouble,
Our World Will Face"

Queen Venetia carefully rolled the parchment, wrapped the twigs around and replaced it in the pouch.

"As you have heard," she continued, "the exact whereabouts of the crown is not clear, but I am sure that *'the gems,* for some unknown reason, are *hating their place'* and bringing our *'times of trouble'*!"

"Then we shall find the *Crown of Rasinja* and discover what wrong has befallen it and we will hope and pray that in doing so, *Aqua Crysta* is released from the ills that have befallen *her*..." announced Lepho, standing determinedly to his feet.

"And the people will see that other causes are to blame, and if those can be fixed, Tregarth won't have a leg to stand on!" laughed Jessica.

"We must act quickly! Are you four with me?" asked Lepho.

"We are!" chorused the four children, sure that they could tackle any unknown hardships which might lie ahead.

"Don't forget we have this to help us!" said Jessica, producing from her waterproof pocket, the garland of jay feathers which she had taken from around Strike's neck. She had thought of presenting it to the Queen but now she knew that it was all part of the magic. It had brought good fortune in the end to Jonathan and Jane. It had brought Jamie and herself to Lepho and the Queen...and now it would bring good fortune in their task ahead.

"But where do we begin the search?" asked Jane. "And how do we get out of this place without the guards seeing us?"

The Queen spoke again.

"I am truly grateful that you are prepared to help in this quest to ensure the well-being of *Aqua Crysta* and to dispel the claims of Tregarth. But the task ahead will be even more hazardous than the tasks you braved during your earlier venture!"

"Never mind, Your Majesty!" chirped Jamie. "I know we'll succeed. Don't forget, we want to clear *our* names as well!!"

The Queen smiled.

"When I heard that you'd all been imprisoned, I thought of the parchment's words and realised that you were the only ones who could help. At least I hoped you would help! In fact, I was so confident that you would, I even prepared a sleeping potion from foxglove seeds for the two guards outside the cellar!"

"Then we had better think of a way of giving it to them!" said Lepho.

"Oh, I already have!" laughed the Queen. "They should be deeply asleep by now!"

Laughter filled the cellar, as everyone got ready to leave. The captives could hardly wait to get through the door, and in no time they were following the well hooded and disguised Queen towards the Floss, first having dragged the guards into the cellar and locked them in!

Soon, they were standing on the river's pebbly shore, beneath the towering heights of the Crystal Cavern. The flow of the river's current had already turned so they knew that the *Goldcrest* would be along shortly.

"I'll bid you farewell here and await Captain Frumo," announced the Queen.

She then performed her final magician's trick and produced five small beautifully iridescent jay feathers, one for each of her explorers. Carefully, her slender fingers threaded them into the sandal straps of Jonathan and Jane and into one of the woven boots of Lepho. The remaining two she popped into the wellington boots of Jessica and Jamie.

"Together with your garland, you are now assured of good fortune in your quest for the *Crown of Rasinja*," she added. "I look forward to seeing you next upon your safe return!"

With that, she turned and walked serenely towards the small pier and awaited the golden vessel. She looked back and waved as Lepho lead the others along the boulder strewn path between the Floss and the towering, pale white and pink cavern walls. With their crystals hidden beneath their clothing, so as not to attract attention, the small party hid in a small rocky alcove and waited for the *Goldcrest* to pass.

They hadn't long to wait. The ship's great square yellow sail could soon be seen bobbing in the distance as the vessel glided down the River Floss. She was a splendid sight as she passed her hidden watchers, majestically slowing down to pick up the solitary passenger. Soon, she was away into the distance and Galdo.

'The Island of Galdo'

The explorers emerged from their alcove and watched the square sail vanish around a gentle bend. "I just hope the Queen returns to her throne safely and does not fall prey to Tregarth's trickery," mused Lepho with an anxious, far away look in his eyes. "We will not know for sure until we return," he sighed. "Then the quicker we get going, the better!" said Jamie excitedly, not really aware of Lepho's plan. "Where are we heading for?" asked Jessica, as they began the trek along the river path.

Lepho explained his idea regarding the meeting place of the five caves mentioned in the parchment's words. Apparently, for centuries, there had been fearful talk among Aqua Crystans of a cavern beyond the last cascade in the *Cave of Torrents*...a cavern of such awesome and wondrous size and associated with tales of such awesome and wondrous horror, that no one had dared visit it since the party had gone missing which had originally put the *Crown of Rasinja* in its hiding place. That was during, in Upper World times, the reign of the first Queen Elizabeth, the daughter of Henry the Eighth, the King who had destroyed the Abbey of Whitby in the first place.

Strange, blood-curdling noises had been heard by venturers into the deepest depths of the *Cave of Torrents* over the centuries...so horrific that no one had ever explored beyond the last torrent!

"Although legend has it," concluded Lepho, as the party rested by a large, pink stalagmite beside the path, "that the unknown cavern is the meeting place of five caves which spread from the cavern like the spokes of a cartwheel. And, because of these five arms, the monstrous cavern was christened the *Star Cavern*."

"But if no-one has ever seen the Star Cavern, other than the ill-fated men who hid the crown, how do you know that the five caves meet there?" gasped Jonathan, wiping his brow because of the heat. "That, my friend, is the power of legend!" replied Lepho stroking his ginger beard. "All legends have meaning, with their roots in truth. I have every confidence that the five caves will be there!"

Jessica and Jamie had sailed past the entrance to the *Cave of Torrents* on their journey between Pillo and Galdo on their summer visit. They knew it to be about halfway between the two and although they'd only glimpsed it as the Goldcrest had sped by, their memories of it were crystal clear. Now, they were really looking forward to seeing it at close quarters.

"We will break for a rest and refreshments at *Torrent Lodge* which lies a little way along the length of the *Cave of Torrents*," announced Lepho. "We will be well and truly exhausted by the time we reach there and glad of the hospitality of Megan Magwitch and her daughters!"

The rough, narrow path wound on and on, hugging the Floss, rising and falling, twisting and turning to avoid the large crystal studded boulders and pink stalagmites. Feet began to ache and muscles began to strain, and, together with the warmth, tiredness began to creep over the tiny party which was dwarfed by the enormous cavern. Above them, its sheer walls soared skywards to a roof mostly hidden by swirling clouds of white mist skewered by threatening, pointed stalactites. It was a gloriously awe inspiring sight for which any tourist operator in the Upper World would have given anything to get his hands on! Nothing could possibly match it up there! Jessica and Jamie imagined cable-cars and chair-lifts swinging on wires in the mists and whitewater rafting down the Floss! 'Crystal World' would be the World's Number One tourist attraction...of that they had no doubts!

It was thoughts such as these that filled the minds of the pair as they trudged along, mixed with thoughts about the impossibility of it all, their first Christmas at *Deer Leap,* the unknown Star Cavern and Queen Venetia back at Galdo by now.

Eventually, they arrived at the gaping mouth of the *Cave of Torrents*. The view as they turned the corner was stunning. The long tunnel was packed so tightly with crystals in its milky white walls, that it was probably the brightest and lightest place in the whole of *Aqua Crysta*. Small waterfalls, like steps, stretched as far as the eye could see, each glistening in the crystal light, and, strangely, it was very quiet, considering the number of cascades. Instead, the water seemed to tunefully trickle down the glowing staircase before joining the Floss and heading off to either Lake Serentina at the Galdo end of the main cavern or to the Pillo end...depending, of course, upon which way the river was flowing!

Clustered around the junction of the two caverns were several Aqua Crystan houses either hollowed out of the soaring pink walls or some of the conical, smooth-topped stalagmites that stood by the rivers. But no one seemed to be at home.

"Probably all at one of Tregarth's treacherous meetings!" mumbled Jonathan.

In fact, the only sign of movement was the large waterwheel next to a crystal grinding mill on the edge of the hamlet.

"Good Gracious, even Miller Knapweed has left his precious millstones!" gasped Lepho. "That is practically unknown!"

The path narrowed as it threaded its way, slightly uphill, between the small waterfalls which were separated by stretches of calm, smooth water. After the third cascade, the travellers stopped for a rest and bathed their weary feet in the warm water.

"We'll soon be at *Torrent Lodge!*" said Lepho, gathering up his heather coloured cloak around his knees.

"To think that it's winter up there!" laughed Jessica, gazing at the thousands of small, icicle-like stalactites that covered the roof and confident that, whatever happened, she would be back at *Deer Leap* before dawn for the fun of Christmas Day! Like her last visit, it was almost like having a dream without being asleep!

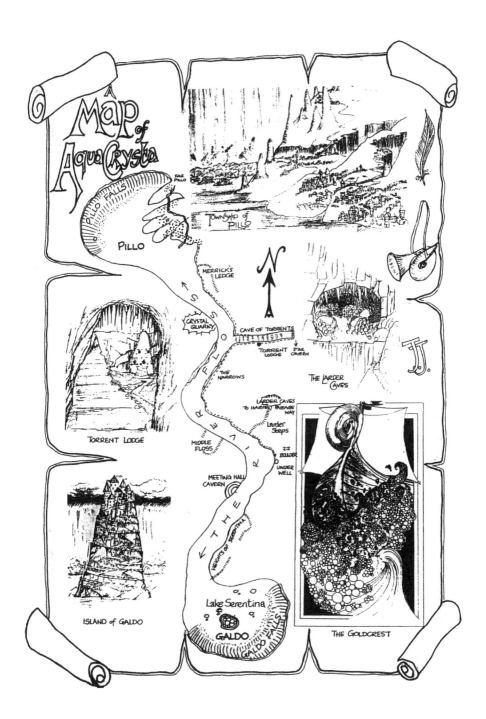

A Map of Aqua Crysta

PILLO FALL'S

FAR PILLO

TOWNSHIP OF PILLO

PILLO

MERRICK'S LEDGE

N

CRYSTAL QUARRY

CAVE OF TORRENTS

TORRENT LODGE

S'AL CAVERN

THE LARDER CAVES

THE NARROWS

LARDER CAVES TO HARVEST PASSAGE WAY

Larder Steps

TORRENT LODGE

MIDDLE FLOSS

J.J. BOULDER

UNDER WELL

MEETING HALL CAVERN

HEIGHTS OF SERENTINA

Lake Serentina

ISLAND of GALDO

GALDO

GALDO FALLS

THE GOLDCREST

J.J.

After the short break, the little group carried on along the path and soon saw *Torrent Lodge* in the distance.

It was a tall, yet stumpy looking stalagmite that had been carved into over the years to make its rooms and passages. Small windows stared back at the approaching party with an almost welcoming expression. The large curved door even seemed to be smiling!

Nearer and nearer they plodded. Now they could see how smooth its walls were caused by centuries of dripping water from a huge stalactite that hung directly above it.

The path lead straight up to the beaming front door which Lepho eagerly knocked, looking forward to the famous hospitality!

There was no reply.

He knocked again, this time harder.

Still no reply. Not a sound.

The place seemed deserted.

"Surely, even if Megan isn't at home, then one of her daughters must be!" cursed a disheartened Lepho. He had pinned all his hopes on food and drink for his band of travellers.

Jamie stepped up to the door and pushed it gently.

To Lepho's amazement it smoothly opened to reveal the inside of the carved out, hollow stalagmite.

Lepho stepped cautiously over the threshold, not quite sure whether he ought to or not. The rest followed, gazing around the magical rooms of the house. All three on the ground floor were beautifully and snugly decorated with all sorts of crystal and wooden objects scattered among the nutshell and wooden furniture. There were cosy, dried moss cushions everywhere, and thick matting made from beaten tree bark but softened with a covering of crushed yellow gorse petals smelling of almonds.

And, of course, every room had its full-sized, colourful jay feathers springing from pots like giant house-plants reaching for the ceilings.

All the rooms were bathed in a gentle, pinkish light from dozens of crystals which gave all the travellers a warm, welcome feeling.

It was indeed easy to see how *Torrent Lodge* had gained its reputation! In the smallest room, Jessica caught sight of a crystal *Sanctum* set, all laid out and ready for two Aqua Crystans to play the chess-like game. She suddenly remembered that she still had one of the pieces from Lepho's set - the minstrel - back in her bedside drawer at *Deer Leap*, together with a quint from the game of *Quintz*. Lepho had given them to her to bring good fortune on their last adventure. He smiled when Jessica tried to apologise for not returning them.

"I have simply replaced them," he said kindly. "You may keep the pieces I gave you as a memento of your first visit!"

It soon became clear that not a single soul was at home, but the table in the main room was set for three. Three wooden goblets, three wooden spoons and three wooden plates were set neatly round the circular rock table. In the centre was a trio of flickering candles in slender crystal candle holders each sending thin, winding plumes of smoke up to the ceiling. Like the candle Jessica and Jamie had seen with Toby and Quentin on the  Larder Cave staircase during their summer visit, there was no sign of melting wax - a reminder of the timelessness of *Aqua Crysta* where nothing aged or decayed.

By the candles were three large bowls each piled high with food of every kind. Toadstool and acorn slices, bramble jellies, dandelion sauce, chestnut fingers, meadow sweet loaf and other delicacies were spilling over the rims of each bowl. It all looked temptingly scrumptious to the hungry travellers, and the jug of cold

oakleaf tea would certainly quench their thirsts!

"Look how some of the plates have got small amounts of food on them as though they'd just started to serve out the food," noticed Jane. "And look at this!" pointed Jonathan, as he bent down to pick up a large wooden serving spoon from the floor with its contents scattered all over the plaited grass mat.

"How peculiar!" said Jessica. "It's as though they were suddenly disturbed just as they..."

"They'll be back soon," Lepho interrupted.

"But why did they leave so suddenly?" asked Jessica.

"I'm afraid I have no answer to your question," admitted Lepho, "but, although it may seem a little ill-mannered, I suggest we replenish ourselves with the morsels before us!!"

"You mean we ought to tuck in and hope they don't mind?" laughed Jamie, eying the feast, his mouth watering.

"Megan is celebrated for her welcome and generosity towards those who travel on foot between Pillo and Galdo," Lepho assured everyone. "She will not mind in the slightest and I will explain our plight on our return."

With that, the unexpected guests began to enjoy the food and drink which lay before them and soon their empty stomachs and dry throats began to recover! Although, it must be added, that they kept glancing through the window, hoping that Megan and her twin daughters would appear.

"How far do we have to go before we reach the last torrent?" asked Jamie between sips of cold tea, and inspecting the crystal carved ornaments on one of the windowsills.

"It is some time since I ventured beyond Megan's lodge," replied Lepho, "but I imagine the walk will be at least as far as we've come already, if not more!"

"What about provisions for the journey?" Jamie inquired, just about to gobble up another spoonful of bramble jelly.

"You're always thinking about your stomach, Jamie!" grumbled his sister.

"No, the young man is correct," said Lepho. "We must take some food and drink from what's left of the meal."

"There won't be much left at this rate if mega-mouth doesn't put a sock in it!" insisted Jessica.

They all laughed...but then Jonathan suddenly stood up.

"Sshh! Listen!" he whispered.

It was the sound of crunching gravel outside.

"Footsteps! There's someone coming!" exclaimed Jessica, running to open the door.

As she grabbed the handle, the door burst violently open and, there, standing before them, was a sight to chill the hearts of all but the most fearless!!

Chapter 7

"Matilda Magwitch!!" exclaimed Lepho, unable to believe the shocking state the young Magwitch daughter was in. Her pale face was scarred and bruised with rivulets of blood and tears running down her cheeks. She was gasping for breath and shaking with fear. Her purple cloak was torn to shreds.

"Help us, please!" she cried as she staggered through the doorway and collapsed at Jessica's feet.

Jonathan and Jamie ran over and helped her to her feet and then, slowly and painfully, she stumbled onto a pile of soft cushions, sobbing uncontrollably. Lepho put a comforting arm around her shoulders while Jane gave her a goblet of tea to sip. Jessica dampened a cloth with water and gently patted her wounded forehead.

"Just rest awhile," whispered Lepho. "You're with friends now. We'll help your mother and sister as soon as we can. But first, try and be calm and then you can us tell where they are and what has happened."

"We must go after them as soon as we can!" sobbed the distressed youngster, who, although she looked the same age as Jessica, was just over a century old in Upper World years. Her pale blue eyes welled with tears as she began to tell her terrible tale.

She told of how the three of them had just sat down to their daily meal when they had heard the most horrendous noise coming from the cave. Megan had opened the door and there, standing by the cascade nearest to their cosy house, was...

Once more, Matilda, began to weep pitifully, unable to bring herself to say what they had seen.

"They s.saw us w.watching them and then about a dozen of them m.made for the house...growling, and roaring and raging as they came closer and closer! Mother slammed the door shut, but the hideous creatures seemed to have the strength of hundreds as they hammered on the door and burst it wide open!"

Matilda wept again as Jessica stroked her frizzy blonde hair.

"We were helpless against such cruel power as their iron arms picked us up and swept us out into the cave. We screamed and beat their enormous muscles with clenched fists. We struggled and kicked, but it was all in vain. We had been captured by the monsters, and they dragged and carried us on and on towards the last torrent! We pleaded for them to let us go but they just bellowed back in a strange language none of us knew."

She stopped and sipped her tea.

Lepho stood and beckoned the others to the far side of the room.

"*Gargoyles!*" he whispered. "They must be *Gargoyles!*"

"But gargoyles are those ugly stone faces outside churches where roofs meet walls!" said Jessica, puzzled by Lepho.

"Like I said earlier, legends are all rooted in truth," Lepho went on, "and believe me, monstrous Gargoyles did, once upon a time, exist in the Upper World...but more of that later...for now, we must be on our way!"

Matilda, too, despite what she had already endured, was eager to follow her sister and mother. Provisions were quickly shoved into every available pocket while Matilda cleaned herself up ready for the journey.

Moments later, Jonathan had closed the front door and the little band was on its way, one behind the other on the narrow path.

The journey to the end of the *Cave of Torrents* was much more difficult than the trek to the lodge had been. For one thing the path was rougher and less well defined, and secondly, because of the increasing heat. It was as though they were approaching a furnace, and Lepho began to wonder if the higher temperatures in *Aqua Crysta* was something to do with heat emerging from the *Cave of Torrents* into the main cavern.

Cascade after cascade they passed with no signs at all of the Magwitches nor their captors. Gradually, the waterfalls became higher and higher, and by a particularly restful and quiet one it was decided to rest. Just below the path was a small inviting crescent of fine, pale pink sand.

Everyone clambered down the shallow bank and jumped into the welcome softness. It was certainly a relief for the feet after the hard, stony path.

At first, the sand was smooth but towards the far end of the crescent it seemed to have been disturbed.

Jane was the first to notice the footprints.

They were everywhere, churning up the sand and heading off in every direction. Indeed, so disturbed was the sand, it was difficult to spot one single footprint.

"Look at these over here!" called Jonathan, with a note of alarm in his voice.

"These aren't Aqua Crystan footprints!"

The rest gathered around, except Matilda who sat at the foot of the bank, lost in thought.

"Definitely...Gargoyles!" said Lepho, bending down and pointing to a print's deep, round heel indentation and its three clawed toes. Jessica planted her wellington booted foot next to one.

"It's enormous!" she gasped. "It must be three times bigger than my foot!"

"And look where the next one is!" Jamie pointed out, as he lunged forwards with three giant paces to reach it!

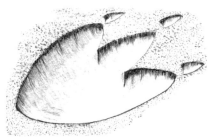

"Obviously the Gargoyles had the same idea as us, and stopped here for a rest!" Jonathan suggested.

It was then that they noticed Matilda who had walked slowly across to them.

"This is where I escaped," she said softly, with a tear rolling down her cheek.

"It's where I saw my mother and Melita for the last time!"

"Now, now, now, don't go saying that, Matilda," said Lepho. "We'll find them. Mark my words!"

"And *when we do*...!" encouraged Jamie, swishing, as usual, his imaginary sword.

He was interrupted by Jane, who was standing by a white boulder on the edge of the sand.

Scratched into the boulder were two words, scrawled roughly with a sharp stone which lay discarded in the soft sand. Jane traced the words carefully with her index finger.There was a longer word and then a shorter one below.

"S...A...V...E.......U...S!!" she spelt.

"And what's that say beneath them?" asked Jonathan, tracing more letters near the bottom of the boulder.

"R...A...S...I..." he spelt out.

But then the letters stopped.

"That doesn't make any sense!" his sister sighed.

"Yes, it does!" burst Jamie, swishing his sword again. "R...A...S...I...*Rasinja, of course!*"

"That's what they kept on saying!" sobbed Matilda, sadly picking up the small sharp stone and imagining the last to hold it. *"Rasinja, Rasinja, Rasinja*...no other words made any sense, but they kept on growling *Rasinja, Rasinja, Rasinja*, as though they were in some kind of magical trance!"

She carefully placed the stone in her pocket and walked slowly away.

"We must make haste!" ordered Lepho. "We cannot afford to lose any more time! If we find the Magwitches then we find the *Crown!*"

"And the *Gargoyles!*" shuddered Jessica.

With renewed energy and spirit the travellers marched along the path passing countless more cascades, each higher and noisier than the one before. Every so often, Lepho related small episodes of the Gargoyles' legend, until Jessica and Jamie had a fairly clear idea who, or rather what, they were!

Apparently, ever since the founding fathers of *Aqua Crysta* had settled in their subterranean world after fleeing the ravages of King Henry Tudor, inhabitants of the Cavern had often considered the possibility of other peoples living below their world. Legend had it that remnants of an ancient, grotesque, goblin-like species lived way beneath the Crystal Waters.

Once, they had roamed the Upper World. Throughout the first millennium, they had terrorized the Romans, the Ancient Britons, the Saxons and the Normans alike, but for some unknown reason had retreated underground shortly after the Norman Conquest in the Upper World year of 1066.

It then became fashionable to put stone gargoyle faces on churches in villages and towns to ward off evil spirits. No sight nor sound of a living gargoyle had been seen nor heard for centuries...but the legend lingered on and had chilled the hearts of young Aqua Crystans at campfire storytimes for many a harvest!

Jessica and Jamie glanced first at one another and then at the giant footprints in the soft sand. Surely these couldn't be the tracks of ancient monsters that once roamed Britain? Neither of them had even heard of them, although they had come across the ugly, stone faces on old churches. Was it all just a legend? But then again...what had made the footprints?

They were soon to find out!

At last the travellers arrived at the final and grandest torrent. The roar of the falling water echoed all around the narrowest part of the cave, and water spray filled the warm air. Soon everyone was soaked as they made their way along the slippery path. Lepho beckoned his followers forward as the path actually disappeared behind the towering waterfall. Everyone's breath seemed to be taken away as they gingerly shuffled along only inches from the rushing, deafening curtain of water. When they emerged at the other side, they just had to sit, gather breath and fight the dizziness that had overwhelmed everyone.

Above them was a staircase cut into the pale rock leading to the top of the waterfall. After the brief rest they climbed the steps which were surprisingly dry despite being so close to the torrential waterfall. The noise became even louder as they reached the last few steps, so loud that Jessica thought she was almost being crushed by the sound. Eventually, everyone reached a small, flat balcony that overlooked the top of the last torrent and beyond down the whole length of the *Cave of Torrents*. The view was spectacular, with the crystal light illuminating all the stepped waterfalls as far as the eye could see...almost to *Torrent Lodge*!

At the other end of the balcony shelf was a rugged opening into a dim passage, lit only by a few crystals embedded in its arched walls. A current of warm air caressed their damp faces as they left the brilliance behind and entered what Lepho worryingly called, 'unfamiliar territory'!

The passage roof was only just a little above Lepho's head as he lead the way, and with outstretched arms the children could easily touch both walls at once. It was certainly different from the main *Floss Cavern* and the *Cave of Torrents*!

Jamie shook and cursed his useless torch, but at least the Queen's crystals helped light the way through the passage.

They walked on and on, until, in the distance they could just make out a strange cluster of twinkling, violet lights hovering calmly one moment and then darting about crazily the next.

The party stopped and stared.

"They're beautiful!" gasped Jessica.

"But, *what* are they?" asked Jamie.

Lepho, unusually, was standing there with his mouth wide open, seemingly even more amazed at the sight before them.

"*Crystalids!*" he whispered, his voice quivering with excitement. "I can hardly believe it!"

"You mean like the ones in the museum at Pillo?" said Jane. "Those that were found floating in the Floss, harvests and harvests ago?"

"The very same, but these are *alive!*" beamed Lepho, steadily walking forwards. "Those at Pillo are dead ones, of course, and no one has ever known from where they came!"

The rest of the travellers moved forward as Lepho inched towards the magical, animated constellation

that danced before them. Its colours even began to change, through turquoise, amber, indigo and back to violet. Then, alarmingly, the twinkling swarm headed directly towards its unexpected observers.

"Down! Everyone down!" exclaimed Lepho. "They've been attracted by our crystals! Hide them, quickly!"

Moments later, the strange squadron of flying creatures was hovering directly above the stunned Aqua Crystans and Jessica and Jamie. Would they attack and sting like a swarm of threatened wasps in the Upper World? Or were they just curious and harmless? There was no way of knowing! This was an encounter with a completely unknown species! Perhaps, one of Jessica's heroes - Sir David Attenborough, the television naturalist - would have been just a *little* wary himself!

As the creatures circled, the only sound that could be heard was the gentle buzz of fluttering wing beats. Each crystalid was the shape and size of a glassy humming bird, but totally transparent with its inner and outer, everchanging coloured glow. Yet they weren't birds...more like giant dragonflies, with shimmering, iridescent wings and long beaks. That was it! A cross between a tropical humming bird and a crystal dragonfly!

They seemed quite harmless, and one even landed on Jessica's scarlet bob-cap! She slowly raised her hand towards it and, incredibly and trustingly, the beautifully delicate creature crawled onto her fingers. Its six legs tickled as it explored, its long greeny-blue antennae probing the warm air.

"It's so light!" whispered Jessica.

"And just look at those colours!" whispered Jane. "It's as though its made of crystal pieces all glued together!"

To see the amazing, unknown, crystal insect-bird was indeed a tremendous experience, a privilege, but a moment later, the magic ended as the swarm suddenly took off back into the depths of the dim passage. The dazzling shooting stars faded...and were gone...and the tunnel seemed strangely empty.

The intrepid explorers walked on, all quietly touched by the new magic. By now their clothes and faces were completely dry and it was becoming stiflingly hot in an incessant draught which seemed to blow stronger and stronger as they marched along the passageway.

Then the noise from the *Cave of Torrents* suddenly completely vanished, and was replaced almost instantly by a peculiar, rhythmic humming sound - as though someone had switched on an enormous machine! As they walked on, the humming became louder and louder and a pinkish-red glow in the distance became brighter and brighter.

Then, as they rounded a final gentle bend, they saw before them the full splendour of a disc of glowing red that marked the end of the passage.

The red strangely flickered brighter and fainter almost in time with the humming. With the increasing heat and the bright red glow, it was like approaching the mouth of a giant furnace!

As they neared the ever growing radiance, the humming reached a throbbing crescendo...and then stopped abruptly. The shock made them all flatten themselves against the passage walls, their imaginations conjuring up all sorts of Gargoyles appearing from nowhere. All was silent as they stayed perfectly still, frozen in the heat, hearts beating and faces glowing red.

But then, as suddenly as it had stopped, the humming started again! Everyone breathed a sigh of relief!

The silence had somehow seemed more threatening, as though some*one* or some*thing* had turned off the din...to *listen*!

Lepho beckoned the rest forward and they crept towards the very end of the passage.

The passage just stopped sharply at a flat, rocky edge and the void that yawned beyond was the most magnificent sight any of them had ever seen!

The vast emptiness reached high - twice as high as the *Floss Cavern* - to a smooth domed roof which was the home of hundreds of blood red stalactites and glowing scarlet crystals. But as well as its dizzy heights, the cavern walls plunged deep below the mouth of the passage into fearsome depths, where a forest of blood red stalagmites soared upwards!

Jamie, bravely, or foolishly, teetered on the very edge of the passage and stared around in disbelief. It was staggeringly beautiful, yet eerie and somehow final.

"We've come to a dead end!" said a bewildered Jessica, hoping to catch a glimpse of the crystalids again. "We can't go on, or up or down!"

"But where did the Gargoyles go with the Magwitches?" asked Jane, equally puzzled but at the same time gazing into the splendour of the cavern.

"This, my friends, is the *Star Cavern*!" Lepho announced suddenly. "If you look down beyond the stalagmites you will see four dark cave entrances some distance apart..."

"But I thought there were *five* caves leading from the *Star Cavern*?" asked Jamie quickly.

"Correct, young man," Lepho answered, mopping his glistening brow with his cloak cuff. "The fifth one is directly below, out of our view!"

Jamie leaned as far forward as he dared in the hope of seeing the fifth cave.

"Be careful!" shouted his sister anxiously, but as she called, Jamie stumbled backwards onto the floor of the passage...his torch bounced out of his pocket and rolled towards the vertical drop. Jamie shot a hand out to stop it, but it disappeared over the edge like a rabbit down a hole!

"That was your fault, Jess! You shouldn't have shouted out!" Jamie snapped angrily.

"Calm down, you two," Lepho called over the din of the humming. "We need to put our heads together and work out where the Gargoyles went!"

It certainly was a mystery! There had been no side passages off the main passage, and there had been no other way out of the *Cave of Torrents*. The Gargoyles and the Magwitches just seemed to have disappeared into thin air!

"Perhaps we missed a door or something behind the last torrent," said Jane.

"Perhaps they didn't go up the steps at all." suggested Jessica. Jamie, who was peeping over the edge of the passage again, suddenly called out.

"Hey, look down there! I can see something moving!"

The others gathered round him and stared down into the forest of stalagmites.

"They're figures!" he shouted.

"The Gargoyles!" exclaimed Jonathan.

"And look, there's my mother...and Melita!" gasped Matilda, overjoyed at seeing the rest of her family again.

"But they're all taller than the stalagmites!" noticed Jessica. "Surely they should be tiny, that distance away!"

"We'll solve that mystery when we find the hidden path down into the Cavern!" said Lepho.

"You mean, there's some kind of secret passage?" asked Jamie, enthusiastically jumping to his feet and feeling the passage walls for some kind of concealed entrance!

With the incessant humming ringing in their ears, everyone began searching along the passage walls for signs of a secret door, but however much they tried nothing could be found in the dark passageway.

"The crystals, of course!" roared Lepho jubilantly. "Cast the light from the Queen's crystals into the passage and we shall soon find what we seek!"
Moments later the passage was brilliantly lit, and it was Matilda who squealed with joy almost immediately.
"Look! I've found the letters "M..E..L" scratched on the wall. It's *Melita*!"
The crystals became one as the others quickly crowded round the scratches in the smooth rock.

"And look, there's a huge triangle of cracks in the wall!" pointed out Jonathan.

In front of them, nearly as high as the wall itself, was a perfect, almost equally sided triangle. Lepho pushed against it with all his strength but nothing budged.

"All together!" he called, and all six shoved and pushed as hard as they could ...but still, nothing moved.

"This must be the secret door, but how do we open it?" sighed Jessica.
Matilda began to sob. Desperately, she began to claw at the edges of the triangle with her fingers.

"If we're delayed much longer we won't know which of the five caves they have gone into!" she gasped. "*We must find a way to open it*!!"

Once again, with as much strength as they could muster, they all pushed against the giant triangle...but it just would *not* move!

"Perhaps it's jammed!" gasped Jessica.

"Or only the strength of the Gargoyles can open it!" puffed Jamie.

Suddenly, the most horrific screeching wail came from the *Star Cavern*!

It was so loud that it even drowned the throb of the humming!

The party froze and listened.

Was it some kind of alarm?

Did the Gargoyles know they were there?

Then came the spine-chilling scream again, this time even louder!

But it was the next sound that sent shivers of fear through the travellers!

A sound the like of which none of them had *ever* heard!

The angry, growling roar of some kind of creature!

Chapter 8

"I'm going back to look into the *Star Cavern!*" shouted Jonathan. "Whatever's making that din is down there!" As he ran off from the rest, he suddenly tripped and fell headlong along the passage. His foot had caught in a metal ring almost flush with the rocky floor. It was about as wide as a dinner plate.

"That's it!" exclaimed Jamie. " Forget the racket down there, that's how we get through the door! We've got to pull the ring!"

Lepho, Jonathan and Jamie pulled with all their might and slowly but surely the ring moved, and then from a small carved hole in the rock under the ring, two huge chain links emerged, rusted with age.

"The door's moving!" yelled Jane. "It's sliding further into the wall!" Then three...four...five more links appeared, as the great triangle of rock slid with a deep grating sound into the wall.

"I can see red light around the edges!" called Jessica. "Keep pulling!" More rusty links appeared and soon a dozen or more links stretched tightly from the hole to the ring. More and more light shone around the edges of the triangle.

"The gap's wide enough for us to get through!" shouted Jessica.

Once more, the earth shattering roar filled the air.

Lepho, Jonathan and Jamie dropped the ring and ran as fast as they could into the huge triangular space in the wall.

"Follow me!" called Lepho, as he slipped through the bright red gap.... unaware that the chain-link snake was also slipping slowly back into its hole, dragging the metal ring behind it.

Jessica followed Lepho, then Matilda and Jane.

"The door's closing!" yelled Jane.

Jamie tried to get through, but the gap had shrunk.

"Stand back, Jamie! You'll get crushed!" shouted Jessica.

Relentlessly, the vast rock triangle slid back towards the passage.

"Quick, grab the ring!" shouted Jonathan.

The metal ring was inching along the floor as the links vanished below the floor.

They both grabbed it, but however much they pulled, the door just kept on closing...and closing...the chain links disappearing one by one.

"It's no use!" panted Jamie letting the ring fall to the floor. The last two links crept away, the ring stopped moving...and the door was shut fast!!

They both collapsed to the ground, exhausted, as another monstrous roar resounded through the passage.

Meanwhile, Lepho and the girls were frantically trying to find another ring to pull on the other side of the door.

"There must be some way of opening the door from this side!" pleaded Jessica almost hysterically, as she ran her fingers over the rock searching for a lever, a ring...anything that would shift the door!

Yet another thunderous roar filled the passage, so piercing this time that Jonathan and Jamie cowered by the wall of the passage and covered their ears.

Then, to their horror, a dark, sinister shape began to appear at the end of the tunnel, silhouetted menacingly against the blood red.

Both boys were speechless as the indistinct shape gradually grew and then finally extinguished the bright redness of the

Star Cavern. All at once they were plunged into darkness! They held their crystals aloft to shed light down the passage...and what they saw made them gasp with terror!

The shape was alive!

It was an enormous head, covered in gleaming scales. It had two flaring nostrils and two staring bulging, black eyes. Suddenly, a mouth opened like a cavern itself, revealing rows of glinting, pointed white teeth like stalactites and stalagmites. Then, worst of all, a great glistening tongue shot out from between the teeth and reached along the passage towards the boys!

Its sticky, dripping tip crawled and squirmed along the passage as though it had a life of its own. Then it slithered back into its cave. The creature rolled its head back, opened its mouth, and ear shattering thunder shook the passage. Jonathan and Jamie felt the floor and the walls shake. Crystals shook and sharp fragments of rock fell from the roof. It was as though an earthquake had struck!

The monster's eyes stared wildly down the passage. Its nostrils flared with anger and its mouth gaped open again!

Once more the writhing serpent of a tongue crept towards its prey, like that of a lizard delving into an ants' nest. It reached its furthest extent, its slimy, glistening tip weaving in the air, straining for blood!

The boys, paralysed with fear, gazed at it creeping nearer...and nearer! Would it reach them?

Would they be plucked from the passage and whipped towards the vicious teeth, like flies caught by a chameleon?

Just then, making them both completely jump out of their skins, they could hear...a *second monster*!...the grating of the door behind them!

They quickly scrambled to their feet, grabbed their crystals and pushed on the rocky triangle for all they were worth! Slowly, oh so slowly, it sank into the wall...and then, to their utter relief, they could see the crack widen around the edge, the bright red light...and then familiar faces!

At last the gap widened just enough for them to squeeze through. Once on the other side they sank to the floor, their chests heaving and their hearts thumping in their ears like the pistons on a steam engine. The nightmare was over...or, was it just *beginning*?

Matilda had thankfully found the ring on that side of the door, and together, Lepho and the girls had pulled on it to move the great triangle of rock. This time it had moved towards them in a wide trough cut into the floor until it was standing totally away from the wall like a huge wedge of cheese.

As Jonathan and Jamie recovered from their ordeal, the door sank back into the rock, grating noisily. Soon, they could just about make out its triangular outline on the wall.

"It's like something out of an Egyptian pyramid!" suggested Jessica, quite amazed by the workings of the door.

"Well, what's on the other side is like something out of '*Jurassic Park*'!!" whispered Jamie to his sister, not wanting to scare Matilda with the rest of her family down in the *Star Cavern*. For the moment, it would be better to say nothing at all about the creature. Jessica looked at her brother and Jonathan. In the red light, she could see the fear in their eyes as they looked at the rocky triangle, their minds full of what they had seen on the other side. She began to wonder if they were doing the right thing. Should they be back home, at *Deer Leap*, curled up snugly in bed waiting for Christmas Day? What dangers was she putting her brother in? Should they make their way back into *Aqua Crysta*, at least? But then she looked at the state Matilda was in, and thought about Queen Venetia losing her throne to Tregarth.

They *had* to carry on! They just *had to*!!

It was beautifully peaceful on this side of the door. It was still hot, but there was hardly a sound. If they listened intently they could just about hear the humming, but at least they couldn't hear the roars they'd heard back in the passage.

They seemed to be on a wide rocky shelf with another deep drop beyond its edge. But this time, an apparently never ending staircase made from ornately carved wood wound downwards clinging to the cliff face, disappearing from view into clouds of swirling pinkish mists. Beyond the mists they could make out the red glow again... presumably light from the *Star Cavern* in the fifth cave.

They began the descent, anxious to catch up with the Gargoyles and the Magwitches, although Jonathan and Jamie were doubly anxious about a certain inhabitant of the cavern! So much so, they decided to lead the way!

The staircase's handrail was wonderfully carved and smooth with whole masses of carved wooden leaves and branches holding it up. Each wooden step was perfectly level. It all looked brand new with hardly any signs of wear, although, judging by the rusty nails, it had been there for many years.

Down and down they went and gradually they all began to notice that the steps seemed to be getting larger, with a greater drop between each one.

Also, they noticed the handrail seemed to be higher, the further they descended!

Eventually, they had to jump between steps and it became impossible to reach the handrail, even for Lepho!

The mists began to swirl around their feet and soon they were completely engulfed in what was almost thick cloud. At one stage it became so thick they could hardly see the next step...and then, mysteriously, the steps seemed to return to the same dimensions as they'd been at the top of the staircase...and the handrail became reachable again!

"Most peculiar!" muttered Lepho, as he stepped off the last step and joined the others in the cave. "It is as if we have grown to match the size of the last part of the staircase!"

"But that's not possible!" laughed Matilda.

"It is as if the mists are the same as the mists which lie under Old Soulsyke's well!" suggested Jamie. "I'm sure we have grown! Follow me and I'll prove it!"

After just a few steps they entered the red vastness of the Star Cavern, which, while still awesome, was nowhere near as huge as it had seemed from the end of the passage. A rough, gritty track wound between the shoulder-high, blood red stalagmites heading for the largest of the four cave entrances that could be seen around the edge of the cavern's floor.

Way above, countless threatening, red stalactites seemed to pierce the ceiling, poised as if to spear the floor at any moment.

"Look up there!" pointed Jamie, inwardly very relieved that there was no sign of the monstrous creature. "It's the end of the first passage, with the hidden door!"

Half way up the precipitous wall was the dark ledge over which they had gazed when they had reached the dead-end. Jamie quickly knelt down and began to feel the rocky track as though he was searching for something. Frantically he ran his fingers over the rough surface completely puzzling the others.

"Is this what you're looking for?" Jonathan suddenly exclaimed, with his hand outstretched.

Nestled on his palm between the life-line and the fortune-line was a tiny glint of silver, so tiny it was amazing that Jonathan had even seen it.

"There's the proof!" beamed Jamie. "It's my torch!"

Carefully, he took the sliver of silver between his thumb and forefinger and examined it, and then placed it gently in his pyjama pocket.

"Then you are correct, my friend!" admitted Lepho. "We *have* grown!"

Gingerly, he felt his arms and legs, never having experienced these proportions in his entire life.

"But, I don't feel any different!" he exclaimed.

"Neither did we when we jumped through the mists at the bottom of the well!" said Jessica.

"Or when we climbed up the rope back into the well last summer!" added Jamie.

"So you think that when we return up the staircase we will shrink back to Aqua Crystan dimensions?" asked Lepho.

"I do!" insisted Jamie, marching off down the track enthusiastically. "But before then we have tasks to complete, *so let's get going!*"

The gritty path wound on and on through the rocky forest until, eventually, the highest, arched cave entrance loomed majestically above them. The warm, red and pink crystal light of the *Star Cavern* gave way to an unwelcoming, gloomy, dim light - made even more unwelcome by the steadily increasing, pulsating, humming sound which seemed to be coming from wherever this cave lead.

Darker and darker, louder and louder, warmer and warmer the journey became, the only relief being the gradually steepening slope downwards of the cave floor.

At first the slope was quite gentle and hardly noticeable, but by the time they had left the *Star Cavern's* glow behind, the way through the cave had become almost a steep, stony scramble, where care had to be taken to avoid falling forwards.

The rough, rocky passage was quite featureless, with just dark greyish, gritty walls. Every so often, Lepho would carefully slip his crystal from beneath his robe to cast light on the surroundings and then quickly conceal it again in case its brilliance betrayed their presence. Although it must be said that there was no sign at all of the Gargoyles and their captives...not even a clue that they'd even passed through the cave before them.

It was just as they were beginning to have doubts that they were on the right path, or they'd missed another secret door, that Matilda noticed the shimmer of a pale blue handkerchief purposely wedged in a thin cleft in the cave wall.

"It's *Megan's*!" she exclaimed in a strange voice coloured at the same time with both sadness and hope.

Jessica put an encouraging arm around her shoulders, and after a short rest perched on ledges by the path, they continued downwards towards what Jamie insisted would be the Centre of the Earth!!

"All I can say is that I'm glad we're full size!" he remarked. "If we'd still been Aqua Crystan size, this part of the journey would have taken forever!!"

Jonathan, who was leading the way, suddenly stopped as he scrambled round a particularly steep bend. His followers, too, all halted and stared into the near distance.

A strange, eerie, pale green glow, almost fluorescent, gently illuminated the way ahead, casting its spooky hue on the travellers' faces.

"Jess, for goodness sake, pull your bobcap down over your face!" joked Jamie. "You look like a spook you'd see in a fairground ghost train!"

"And so do you-ooo!!" his sister laughed, raising her arms like a phantom in a graveyard.

The further they descended, the brighter the green radiance became and the louder the humming throbbed in their ears. But gradually, the cave's path became less steep and progress became considerably easier. Indeed, the way ahead soon became almost horizontal much to the relief of their tired legs.

It was then that they began to notice strange, discarded trucks littering the cave floor on each side of the path. Some were on their sides, some upside down, but they all consisted of four rusty, chunky, iron wheels at each corner of a deep, wooden, open-topped box about the size of the bath back at *Deer Leap*. Each had a kind of towing chain attached to one end, and it seemed that each pair of front wheels could swivel on a central pivot for guiding the truck when pulled.

"They're like coffins on wheels!" suggested Jamie, as he spun one of the wheels of an upside down truck.

"I wonder what they were used for?" Jane asked.

"This could be the answer!" called Jonathan from behind a precariously balanced heap of half-a-dozen or more wrecked trucks. He was tugging at something with all the strength he could muster, but whatever it was, was out of sight to everyone else.

"What on earth is it?" shouted Jessica. "Be carefu....!"

But it was too late!

With an almighty jolt, Jonathan suddenly fell backwards, at the same time swinging uncontrollably an enormous pickaxe almost as big as himself!

Then one of its great arched prongs swung into the lowest truck in the pile...the huge heap began to wobble...it swayed to one side...and then the whole lot toppled across the path with a crash that would have wakened the dead!

At once, the throbbing hum stopped as though a switch had been thrown!

Instinctively, everyone scattered and hid in any crevice they could find in the cave walls.

The complete silence that followed was so solid that it was almost touchable.

Thoughts rushed through the minds of the hidden explorers.

Hearts raced.

Surely the clatter of the collapsing trucks had been heard.

The eerie green, silent brilliance suddenly flickered.

Slow, determined crunching footsteps echoed in the distance!

Nearer and nearer!

Then to the horror of the hidden, staring, petrified eyes, dark shadows crept along the rocky floor like a menacing, moonless tide in a sea-cave.

The silent, shadowy swash broke over the wrecked wood and wheels...and then...stopped.

Breaths were held tightly in the crevices of the cave.

Would they be seen?

Would they, too, be captured by the hideous Gargoyles?

Would they *ever* return to *Aqua Crysta*?

Chapter 9

For what seemed like an eternity, the two arms of the black, shadowy tide halted. Then, they merged into one dark pool...and retreated, as though drawn back by the pull of an invisible moon. Soon they had melted into the greenness and were gone together with the fading footsteps.

Lepho breathed a sigh of relief and signalled to the others to slowly emerge from their hiding places. One by one, like hermit crabs leaving their shells, they cautiously stepped into the brilliant green of the cave.

"The coast seems to be clear!" whispered Lepho, as loudly as he dared.

"That was a close shave!" whispered Jessica. "If we'd been seen, that would have been that!"

"No more tampering with pickaxes!" Lepho warned Jonathan, though with a grin lighting his face beneath his knitted, ginger eyebrows. Jonathan knew he had been foolish.

Without any further ado, Lepho beckoned his followers forward and they stole into the green, like moonlit, midnight cats...almost on tiptoes in the eerie silence.

After a few tentative steps, the silence suddenly ended as sharply as it had begun. The humming returned. This time, louder than ever.

Somehow, though, it was welcome, as it cloaked and masked their presence.

They gingerly rounded a gentle bend and, to their relief, there was no sign at all of the owners of the two great shadows. Instead, what met them was the full glare of the origins of the green brilliance. Now, instead of casting an eerie light, it was of dazzling brightness. Eyes were quickly shielded.

It was almost like staring at a blazing summer sun...and its radiant heat was scorching. The whole end of the cave was an indistinct mass of brilliance, so bright that it seemed impenetratable.

With shining faces glistening with beads of sweat, and arms aloft, shielding their eyes, the determined band pressed on into the unknown.

Lepho suddenly stopped and squinted through his fingers into the glare of the emerald sun. There were figures moving, silhouetted against the green. Hunchbacked figures, dragging what seemed to be heavy loads judging by their posture...in trucks with chains, identical to the ones discarded back along the passage. One after the other, all in the same direction, in a continuous procession. Each load was heaped high in each truck. On and on, the straining silhouettes crossed the sun, a never-ending chain of toil.

Meanwhile the humming became louder and the heat became greater. Then the last figure and its truck crossed the brilliant green, stumbling as it went. As the figure tried to scramble to its feet and gather its truck, a much larger, menacing figure appeared from the left, and began to strike the cowering figure with a lashing whip. The cracks echoed down the passage like gunfire as the smaller figure summoned all the energy it could to drag its load after the others. Then the silhouetted savagery vanished from view, as both players departed the brilliant stage. Lepho and the rest had observed a scene of such tragic cruelty, it was hard to believe it had actually happened. It had been like watching some kind of slavery drama at a macabre theatre.

Chilled by what they had seen, they moved on with heavy hearts until they cautiously came to the end of the cave hoping that more figures wouldn't suddenly appear. None did, but what they saw beyond the cave mouth made them all gasp in disbelief!!

The scene before them was an enormous living cauldron. A hive, a bees' nest of frenzied activity within a huge, hollowed out crystalline sphere. Whereas all the caves and caverns of *Aqua Crysta* were tunnel-like with rivers, sheer walls and ceilings packed with stalactites, here was the inside of a sphere of solid crystal!
"It's all been hollowed out by the Gargoyles!" gasped Jessica, in awe at the wondrous sight. "They must have quarried it for centuries and centuries! And look, there are crystalids flying all over the place!"

The vast, curved expanse of raw white crystal, made green by the glow, covered every square inch of the inside of the almost perfect sphere, except for the maze of white criss-cross tracks that scarred its surface. Everywhere, Gargoyles with pickaxes and trucks were slaving in the cauldron forever enlarging it. Dotted around were larger Gargoyles acting as overseers, each armed with a whip or stick. Again it reminded Jessica of Ancient Egypt...the slaves quarrying stone for the pyramids.
Against the humming, they could hear the constant tap-tapping of pickaxes on the crystal, but it was what stood at the centre of the cauldron's floor that was the most awesome.

For there, in its resplendent majesty, was an enormous, golden crown, every detail of its ornate, intricate, eastern design picked out by the green shimmering light. To Jessica it spoke of Turkish temples and spiring minarets in ancient Mesopotamia. Its sheer size was staggering - at least five or six times taller than the nearest Gargoyle - but it was the countless green gemstones embedded in its lustrous gold that captivated its observers the most. These, incredibly, were the sole source of, not only the green radiance but also of the heat and the throbbing, rhythmic humming!

The surface of every single emerald was a moving kaleidoscope of smooth, brilliant, dazzling faces - all seemingly alive, flickering with some kind of mystical inner life and energy. Every gemstone held its own fiercely raging fire, with fiery, green flames licking the insides of the glassy, verdant cauldrons. They were burning so ferociously it seemed as though the flames were trying to escape their torment, to break out of their crystalline cellars.

And what's more, all the flames acted in unison, as though choreographed by some invisible fiery dance-master. A thrust of the flames within every emerald was followed by a retreat, a summoning of energy, then another thrust, each producing the pulsating, throbbing hum.

The whole scene held the small band of travellers spellbound. They were totally captivated by the huge, hollowed out crystal sphere, the incessant activity of the Gargoyles, but most of all by the gargantuan *Crown of Rasinja*. It was like a queen bee in the middle of a hive, somehow totally dominating everything.

Truck after truck of quarried white crystal arrived at a huge, sugary mound around the base of the gigantic, emerald encrusted crown. Each truckload was tipped onto the mound and as the white crystals merged with the heap of green, they too glowed the same green as the giant emeralds towering above them.

"But what are the Gargoyles doing?" burst Jamie at last. "Why are they piling up all this crystal around the crown? Are they trying to bury it?"

"And why is it so large?" asked Matilda, wondering how on earth they were going to find her mother and sister in all this mayhem.

"And why is it humming and so hot?" Jonathan chipped in.

Lepho had no answers this time, but just stared at the magnificent sight before him. They all stared as if transfixed by

the crown's magical power. They seemed powerless to move.
All thoughts of the dangers of being seen evaporated as they were held
in its grasp. They were trapped by an invisible force. Rooted to the spot
by the awesome wonder of this hidden world which lay beneath *Aqua
Crysta* and within the Earth like a buried, living, inside-out planet from
another galaxy!

But, unknown to them, their dreamlike state of
wonder was about to end as they were all abruptly jolted back into
reality!
Each of the six travellers, at one and the same time, suddenly felt
rough, heavy hands grasp their shoulders in vice-like grips.
They had been seen...and quietly, despite their bulk...a gang of giant
Gargoyle overseers had crept up on them...and *grabbed their prey*!!

Jessica and Jamie, and the Aqua Crystans had been
like moths to a lamp. The radiance of the ancient emerald studded
crown had worked its magic...but now its Gargoyle keepers had to
make sure that these intruders from other worlds would *never* return
to their Lands to tell of their discovery!
Never!!

Chapter 10

As each of the prisoners slowly turned, their horrified eyes fell, for the first time, upon the full, hideous sight of the Gargoyles! The encounter would remain with the captives for the rest of their lives, and come time and time again to haunt them on the darkest of nights.

Jabbering away in a language foreign to any of their prey, the monsters' heads had a harsh reptilian scaliness. Lipless mouths hardly moved as they spoke in deep, croaky tones. The mouths were wide, almost from stubby ear to stubby ear, straight and featureless, like those of snakes. It was almost as if darting, forked tongues would suddenly appear, but none did. Above the mouth of each Gargoyle was a flattened broad nose with flaring, wide nostrils. But it was the eyes that sent waves of fear down the spines of the prisoners. Bulging, unblinking, stony, lifeless eyes with black, horizontal, slit-like pupils set in colourless irises. As icy cold and hostile as you could imagine. No twinkles, no smiling eyes here! Not even eye-lids or eyelashes to soften their harshness. They seemed to be pure stone.

Above their broad, rough,wrinkled foreheads, which yielded not a drop of sweat despite the heat, were waves of almost solid, sculpted hair, set sweeping backwards with central partings.

They were virtually neckless, with their angular, hard chins merging into wide, very wide, chests which billowed with rank upon rank of gristle and solid muscle.

Bulbous, powerful shoulders sprouted short, stocky arms, packed with biceps the size of rugby balls. In turn these boughs branched beyond broad wrists into shovel like hands with three gnarled fingers, and a thick thumb, each tipped with a viscious claw.

The rest of their bodies were out of sight from the captives as they were held rigid, but as they were pushed and shoved down one of the truck tracks, they could see their shortish, muscle bound legs gradually tapering into stubby three-toed feet, again tipped by sharp, thick claws. They wore nothing but short, greyish, coarse loin cloths.

Besides their stony ugliness, the thing that struck everyone the most, was their skin. It looked like set cement with rough grooves like the bark of an oak tree. In fact, their whole powerful, stiff, unyielding character was very tree like.

They'd been captured by speaking, animated oak trees!

Each towered well above Lepho, so he, as well as the rest, were unable to break free, even if they'd wanted to. But it seemed useless to try. The shock, the unreality of these alien creatures, the staggering nature of the quarry, the heat, the noise, the activity had all overpowered the travellers as much as the Gargoyles. It was futile to struggle.

Still jabbering, excitedly in their strange croaky, clicking language, the six overseer Gargoyles and their prisoners made their way down the white track towards the emerald inferno. Groups of smaller worker Gargoyles pointed, stared and chattered as they momentarily looked up from their quarrying before being barked at by the overseers.

Single worker Gargoyles, dragging empty trucks up the white track, glanced stiffly, sadly up from the ground, as they passed the captives. One of them was the weaker, particularly bent worker they had witnessed being beaten by the overseer in silhouette earlier.

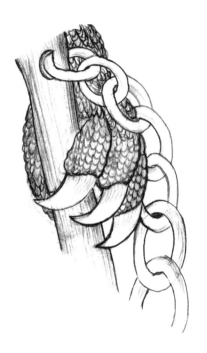

Once again, as he passed, the Gargoyle gripping Jonathan lashed out at the worker with a clenched fist. The blow knocked the ailing Gargoyle off his feet and he stumbled into a heap of crystals before staggering on up the track with his truck. It was then that Jessica noticed that his truck's chain was fixed to his wrist by an iron band. Indeed, all the workers who dragged the trucks were bonded to them. Jessica suddenly felt sadder for their plight than for her own. She had read about slavery in her history books, but never dreamed of witnessing such savagery!

The white, crushed crystalline track wound round to the floor of the gigantic, white sphere. By now, the full majesty of the visible part of the enormous *Crown of Rasinja* soared above Jessica, Jamie and the Aqua Crystans. Still held fast in the grip of the Gargoyles and speechless by a mixture of wonder and fear, they gazed up into its fiery jewels set in their field of beaten, gleaming gold.

Each of the smooth, glassy faces of the magnificent gemstones was alive with flickering energy. The green flames could now be seen dancing and darting, trapped in their transparent pyramids. Crystalids flew all around like insects at a honey pot, each crystal creature reflecting the green light as well as radiating its own colours.

The heat was now almost unbearable, scorching the faces of the captives.

The Gargoyles seemed cool and untouched by it, their vice like grips unrelenting as their prey tried to shield themselves.

To the relief of their prisoners, the Gargoyles marched onward, beyond the raging crown. But what loomed ahead filled the eyes of the captives and doubled their living nightmare!
A vast void in the floor of the crystal sphere!
A perfectly circular hole, at least as wide as a tennis court.
A pit.
How deep, no one could imagine.
Were they going to be thrown alive into the fiery bowels of the Earth?
Was this the end?
Were they at the doorstep of Hell?

Two taut chains with large oval links emerged vertically from the gaping hole. Each one wound over a long, solid, horizontal cylinder, the size of a tall, felled pine tree.
Then each chain stretched downwards at an angle to where they wrapped around an enormous windlass, with huge turning handles at each end.
It was as though something was regularly raised and lowered up and down the hole.
Nearer and nearer the six were shoved and pulled, until they were held fast on the pit's very edge.
As thoughts of plunging to their deaths flashed through all their minds, Matilda suddenly let out a scream of joy that surprised even the Gargoyles! At once, they stopped jabbering, as the Aqua Crystans gazed down at what was in the pit.

There were no bottomless depths after all!!
Instead, there was a circular floor, flush with the walls of the hole, save for a small gap all the way round. It was just a jump away from the edge......and sitting in the centre...in a close huddle...were Megan Magwitch and her daughter, Melita... together with three glaring Gargoyles!
Matilda again shrieked with all her might, and struggled and kicked. So much so that her Gargoyle released his grip and let her jump down

onto the circular floor to join the rest of her family. A moment later all three, with their blonde, frizzy hair and heather coloured gowns decorated with floral motifs, became a single, entwined knot of happiness. With much hugging and kissing and weeping they were reunited, while the Gargoyle guards looked on bewildered by this unknown emotion. They seemed as stony cold inside as well as out.

"We thought we'd never ever see you again!" sobbed Megan hugging Matilda.

"But who are your friends? Did they rescue you?"

"Wipe your eyes, mother, then you will recognise them!" smiled Matilda.

Megan dabbed her tear-filled eyes with her cuff and looked up.

"Lepho!...Jonathan and Jane!...Jessica and Jamie!"

She stopped and stared at the five, one by one, her face showing signs of confusion.

"But...but Tregarth says you're all guilty of...!" she called.

"Mother, mother, stop!" burst Matilda. "They are innocent! It's the evil Tregarth who is the guilty one! It's a long story, but Queen Venetia has sent them on a quest to prove it!"

Still confused, but relieved at the news and being reunited with her daughter, her face broke into a smile.

"I have always believed it! We have all always believed it!" she beamed.

"But how can we do anything about it here, trapped in these dismal depths with these...*these monsters*?"

"We will find a way!" reassured Matilda, dabbing away her mother's tears with the pale blue handkerchief she had found. "Lepho and his companions will see to that. I know they will!"

At that moment, the Gargoyles on the brink of the hole, roughly pushed their five other captives over the edge. They tumbled in a heap onto the hard wooden floor and the Magwitches ran to comfort them. They had hardly got to their feet when three of the overseer Gargoyles plunged over the edge to join them too!

It was then, with the sudden thud of the heavy Gargoyles landing besides them that all the prisoners noticed that the floor was gently rocking from side to side!

"The floor's floating!" exclaimed Jamie, at once glad to be free of his Gargoyle's grip and amazed at the movement beneath his feet.

"And look at that!" pointed Jane. "There's water splashing over the edge of the floor!"

It was true. All around the edge of the floor, water was lapping!

Slowly, the floor ceased its gentle rocking, and the water receded, leaving a halo of glistening, green dampness around its rim.

"I can smell salt!" said Jonathan, sniffing the air.

"It's like sea-water!" added Jessica. "But that's impossible, we're miles from the sea!"

Suddenly, Jamie pointed to the stone wall surrounding them.

"Look, the wall's moving!" he shouted, "The wall's moving upwards!"

"Or we're moving downwards!" remarked Lepho, watching the three Gargoyles stood at the edge of the hole beginning to shrink.

He was right!

Accompanied by the clanking of the huge, rusty chains as they crawled over the enormous cylindrical beam above them, the floor was slowly sinking into the hole! The surrounding wall became wet and shiny with traces of soggy moss. It was like sinking into an giant, dripping, circular well.

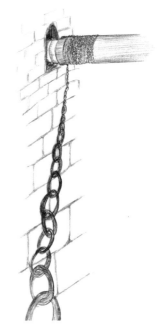

The reluctant passengers gazed at the ever increasing height of the circle of cut stone, as the six Gargoyles stood like statues, their faces grim and lifeless, well aware of what was happening.

Above them, the gleaming green radiance of the white crystal quarry began to fade, together with the heat and the throbbing hum. Gradually, it became cooler and darker, as the floating, circular platform sank further into the unknown depths.

Deeper and deeper.

Darker and darker.

The streaming wet wall glistened in the fading light, until almost total darkness engulfed the voyagers. Soon the top of the shaft was but a greenish moon in a night sky. It was as though they were in the depths of space retreating from a distant planet.

The journey was serenely silent, save for the gentle, soothing lapping of water around and beneath the vessel.

It was so cool and quiet.

Almost relaxing and dreamlike.

Indeed, sleep was almost creeping upon Jessica and Jamie and the Aqua Crystans, as the craft sank silently into the darkness.

Heads began to nod, eyes began to close. Tiredness and the lullaby of gurgling water began to usher in drowsiness and slumber and... sleep...sleep...wonderful slee...

And, of course, wonderful sleep was at large, way, way above the travellers, too! For a start, Mr Dawson was still fast asleep in his bedroom at *Deer Leap*, blissfully unaware that not only was it snowing heavily (which would give him a much dreamed of *White Christmas*!) but also that his two children had once again vanished into one of their secret adventures!

Then there were the animals of the forest. All of them, even the ones of the night, were tucked away beneath the thickening blanket of snow. Just a few had discovered the corridors of warmth that were like brown scars across the white, where fallen cones and shoots of grass could still be nibbled.

The monster-reptile that lurked beneath *Aqua Crysta* was even asleep! Curled in his rocky lair in one of the passages leading to the *Star Chamber* slept the creature. But his sleep was fitful and disturbed. It was too warm for a reptile seeking shut-eye!

The only places where sleep was absent were in the Gargoyles' quarry and in *Aqua Crysta*! Here, her people were restless and uncomfortable, not only because of the heat, but because of the rousing words spoken by Tregarth.

His stirring speeches had been successful, very successful!

Even now, he was marching on the Queen's Palace at Galdo with a horde of discontent Aqua Crystans at his heel.

His reluctant supporters were leaving their crystal homes, market-stalls, peaceful games of *Quintz* and *Sanctum*, their boats on the Floss, their crystal carving and even their tankards of fizzy bramble wine and plates of toasted acorn slices!

It was clear that Queen Venetia was in trouble as she peeped through one of the Palace windows, her fingers playing with a strand of jay feather and only Merrick, the Mayor of Pillo, for company.

"The proof of Tregarth's evil plot will be with us soon!" encouraged Merrick.

"Trust Lepho and the newcomers from the Upper World!"

"I have every faith in my venturers," replied the Queen, "but time seems unusually against us in our usually *timeless* world! I feel its burden!"

Outside the Palace, her people gathered amid the toadstools and the market-stalls. They were not angry nor aggressive. There was no calling or jeering.

But they were heavy in number. Tregarth had been persuasive!

Then, not a crystal's throw from her front door, Tregarth fearlessly climbed onto a market-stall, raised his arms and looked behind him at his followers. He then gazed into the Heights of Galdo. The spiralling pathways that soared to the top of the vast, hollowed-out stalagmite and the swaying aerial walkways that strung across the tapering space between them were packed with Aqua Crystans all silently awaiting his words.

Tregarth began his final address.

"Venetia!" his voice boomed, rattling every single crystal piece on every single *Sanctum* board throughout the Island. "You can see that your people have turned against you! They are now *my people*!! Your reign is over!!"

Queen Venetia opened her door and, together with Mayor Merrick, stood defiantly facing her enemy.
Serenely, as always, she beamed at her people, her golden hair cascading over her green and silver gown, her matching coronet glinting in the crystal light.
"The *Elmwood and Crystal Throne* will never be yours," she said calmly, without even a trace of venom. "The proof that *your* words are false and treacherous will soon be with us all. As I speak, my noble venturers...your former prisoners...are on their..."
"*You jest,* Venetia!" growled Tregarth, his raven eyebrows knitting together, his eyes narrowing, his loyal henchmen looking uncomfortable. "The ones of whom you speak are *imprisoned* beneath the Larder Steps!!"
The Queen smiled...and so did each and every one of her gathered people.
They knew that smile.
And they knew the tide was turning!
The Magic was returning (if it had ever been away!)
The Magic was with their Queen and their kingdom!
Even *Lumina*, the eternal candle-flame was beginning to recover!
Her guardians, Quentin and Toby, also smiled as the flame suddenly soared and plumed.
Tregarth was doomed...but not quite yet!

Deep, deep below, in depths so deep, sleep on the round, floating raft suddenly came to an end! With a jolt that shocked everyone back to their senses...the descent suddenly stopped, with a crash that sounded like the floating floor had landed on some kind of solid surface.

Everyone stirred and rubbed their weary eyes.

A soft, pale green light lit their faces and the frozen faces of their guards.

A gentle, refreshing breeze caressed their hair.

"I can smell the sea!" exclaimed Jessica, stretching her arms and trying to fully awaken.

The Gargoyles, as one, immediately began their feverish, cackling jabber and sprang into life. Barking unknown commands, they hustled their captives towards the edge of the floor, where three or four wide, slippery, stone steps lead into the mouth of a dim, damp cave.

Drips of water fell like rainfall from the low ceiling.

"It's salt-water!" whispered Jonathan, as he licked his lips.

"We're in a sea-cave. We must be near the coast!" Jessica whispered back, "Look at the washed up seaweed on the floor!"

A trickle of water beneath their feet vanished before their eyes and in the distance they could just make out shallow water quickly retreating as though it was draining away.

"It's the tide!" whispered Lepho as loudly as he dared. "We've just floated down on a column of sea-water in the shaft, and now it's ebbing away to the sea through this cave!"

"You mean the Gargoyles have an exit to the sea?" asked Jamie.

"But we can't be anywhere near the sea!" exclaimed Jessica, trying to keep her voice down. "It must be five miles away at least to Whitby and Sandsend!"

"But what about this light? Where's that coming from?" insisted Jamie.

He didn't get an answer, as the Gargoyles suddenly began prodding them towards a strange shape that lay in a large recess at the side of the cave.Whatever it was, was covered in strands of slimy seaweed which the six Gargoyles began to remove as quickly as they could.

Slowly, to the surprise of all their captives, they revealed a heavy, wooden open cart with four enormous, thick rimmed, spoked wheels.

They proceeded to drag it into the main cave, and even more surprisingly, two of the Gargoyles harnessed the other four between two long wooden poles which protruded from the front of the cart. Then they cleared away the last of the seaweed from inside the wagon and herded their prisoners up some ricketty steps and onto two long, damp benches which faced one another. The Magwitches and Lepho sat on one bench, and the four J's sat on the other.

The two Gargoyles then sat at the front and after another round of jabbering chatter, the cart slowly lurched forward along the soggy cave floor.

Jessica took the opportunity to mention the strange light which was gradually becoming brighter.

"The reason why I think we're nowhere near the sea is that the light's not daylight!" she said confidently, now that the rumble of the cartwheels drowned her voice. "It's green, isn't it? In fact, it reminds me of the green light back in the quarry, although it's a lot dimmer!"

"Sis, you're dead right!" admitted Jamie. "But this cave must lead to the sea eventually, yes?"

"I s'pose so, but it's going to take a heck of a time at this speed!"

The cart rumbled on towards the light. The walls of the cave were soaking wet and the ceiling constantly dripped. Soon all the passengers were absolutely drenched, just as though they'd been caught in a rainstorm. Time passed slowly, but it gave Jamie time to think up a load of questions for Lepho.

"If the Gargoyles have got an exit to the coast, how come there have never been reports of ugly monsters roaming around and scaring off holiday-makers on the beaches?" he asked with a smile.

"That I cannot answer, young man!" replied Lepho, wringing out his ginger beard. "But for every question there is an answer, so I am sure we will discover the reason!"

"And what about that floating floor in the shaft?" asked Jamie. "Do you think it moves upwards at high tide? And why, oh why was the *Crown of Rasinja* so enormous? Surely it can't have been that large when the first Aqua Crystans hid it? And why were the Gargoyles piling up all that white crystal around the crown? And why...?" Jessica put a dripping hand over his mouth.

"Jamie, give Lepho a break for goodness sake! You must be driving him mad!"

"Never mind, Jessica," said Lepho, with his hood swept back and water cascading over his freckled face. "All our minds are full of questions. Mark my words, we will answer them all. Just wait and see!"

The cart rumbled on for what seemed like an eternity, but at least the ride gave everyone a rest. The four harnessed Gargoyles seemed tireless as they trudged through the cave, never catching up with the ebbing tide. It seemed, by the wetness of the cave walls and roof, that incoming tides were strong and powerful enough to fill the cave and even force their way up the shaft. When the next high-tide would be no one was sure. They just hoped that the Gargoyles knew what they were doing! The thought of a torrent of water bearing down on them struck fear into the passengers, but they were slightly comforted by thoughts of eventually emerging at the coast, and possibly escaping...although something told them that things wouldn't be quite that straightforward!

The greenness of the light gradually became brighter and brighter, and then suddenly, as they rounded a slight bend, their anxious eyes set upon another spectacular sight!

The cave was flooded with brilliant green - the same green as the green in the quarry from the giant emerald gemstones. But here, it was coming from the cave walls and ceiling. They were completely covered with thousands of tiny crystals somehow embedded into the rock.

As the cart trundled onwards it entered the gleaming tunnel. The passengers and the Gargoyles were bathed in its brilliance, and to the captives' amazement they could feel warmth radiating from the tunnel walls. In seconds they were all completely dry!

"The crystals are the same ones that the Gargoyles were quarrying!" noticed Jessica, emptying out water from one of her wellingtons and gazing at the tunnel walls, which were almost within touching distance.

"But they're green, not white!" puzzled Jane, wringing her pigtails.

"Things are beginning to make some sort of sense!" Lepho calmly pointed out. "The Gargoyles quarry the white crystals, then pile them next to the giant gold and emerald Crown of Rasinja!"

"And then somehow the white crystals become green!" finished Jamie, unfastening his waterproof.

"But how?" burst Jonathan.

"And why have they lined this part of the sea-cave with them?" asked Jessica.

A few moments later, the brilliant tunnel came to an abrupt end, and the cave assumed its normal rocky, mossy nature, once more dripping with salt water. The warm, green glow faded as it was left behind and soon the passengers were soaking again, but their spirits were uplifted as they sensed a familiar soft glow in the distance.

"Daylight!!" exclaimed Jessica, unable to believe her eyes. "We're nearly there!"

It was the first time that she and her brother had seen daylight since Christmas Eve afternoon! The joy of seeing it again and being back in the Upper World made their hearts race with excitement.

"What's that?" burst Jamie, putting a cupped hand to his ear.

A rhythmic roar could be heard in the distance.

"It's the sea! Waves breaking on a shore!" replied Jessica, bubbling with happiness. "I can't wait to see them!"

The cartwheels rumbled onwards...and then, magnificently, they saw beyond the end of the sea-cave...a wonderful half circle of white, fluffy clouds hanging above a clear horizon beyond a huge expanse of choppy, steely grey sea. The cave mouth swelled as they crept closer and closer.

A fresh sea breeze ruffled their hair and they all deeply breathed in the tangy, salty air.

The cart came to a juddering halt and the two Gargoyles on board, turned and stared harshly at their passengers, their faces even more grotesque in the bright daylight. Grunting and growling, they gestured with wildly flailing, stony arms that Jessica, Jamie and the Aqua Crystans should climb down from the wagon. Stiffly, one by one, they all stepped off the back of the cart and gathered in a silent, nervous cluster on the shingle, just a few, tantalising steps from the open, sandy shore.

The other Gargoyles were quickly unharnessed, and then all six beckoned their captives to follow.

As they jostled forward, the crunch of shingle soon faded as their feet sank into soft, golden sand. Sunlight struck their hopeful faces and, as they left the cave's mouth, the full glorious seascape filled their eyes. They had well and truly arrived in the Upper World!

But there was something strange.

Something wasn't quite right!

Something they'd sensed immediately began to shatter their spirits and fill them with dread!!

Chapter 11

It was their noses that sensed the strangeness first, for mixed in with the tang of salt on the breeze...was the smell of burning...burning wood. Then, as their eyes scanned the grey, desolate coast, they noticed, hovering above the land, about two miles away, a vast swathe of churning, thick, black smoke, blotting out the cloudy sky. Below the great billowing curtain of smoke was a magnificent stone building topped with grand arches and towers each lapped by writhing tongues of fire. From them, smoke curled upward to add to the huge cloak that now even dwarfed the splendour of the building.

"It's the Abbey of Whitby, the home of our ancestors!" exclaimed Lepho in despair.

"But how can this be?

This destruction happened nearly five Upper World centuries ago! Such a sight is not for our eyes now!"

"But the Abbey's just a ruin!" gasped Jamie. "Dad took us to have a look at it a couple of months ago. It should be just a few remains of arches and towers not that huge building! It's almost as big as the Houses of Parliament!"

"And look, the tops of the cliffs in Whitby are covered in trees!" burst Jessica,

"There should be loads of houses and hotels!"

The Gargoyles, too, for the first time, looked shocked and puzzled. Their jabbering had suddenly stopped as their stony eyes gazed into the distance.

Then, all at once, they burst into a frenzy of activity, dragging the wagon out of the cave onto the beach, and then quickly herding their bewildered captives back onto their benches. A moment later, all six Gargoyles had positioned themselves between the wooden poles at the front and were drawing the cart forward through the soft sand. They had an urgency about them which alarmed their passengers, as the cart began to pick up speed when its wheels found firmer sand nearer the gently lapping wavelets of the shoreline. Faster and faster the cart sped towards the enormous burning Abbey which towered above the Whitby cliffs...although Whitby itself seemed to have vanished!

Jessica and Jamie stared in disbelief and total confusion at the coast as it flew by in a blurr. They could tell now that the sea cave had emerged at the little village of Sandsend.

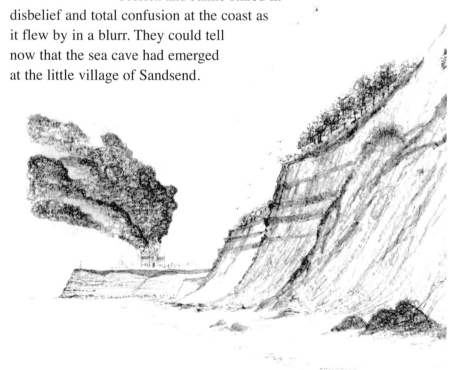

But where were the houses and the hotel?
Where were the little cafes, the old railway station and the car park?
The whole place had just disappeared! There wasn't even a road along
the coast to join it to Whitby! The only sight that looked familiar was
the great, sweeping stretch of sand and pebbles that linked where
Sandsend should have been to the vast, burning Abbey!

      Suddenly, the cart swerved to the right, almost
throwing everyone from their seats. Ahead, running and stumbling
towards them on the beach, was a frantic figure dressed in a long,
flowing, hooded cloak.
He seemed to be shouting and wildly waving and pointing into the
trees that bordered the sand, landwards, where the road to Whitby
should have been.

The next moment, three chestnut horses appeared from amid the tangle of branches and bushes, each mounted by a helmeted rider.

The hard-driven horses sprang as one onto the sand and galloped after the weakening, cloaked figure as he staggered towards the Gargoyles' wagon. With tails and manes flying in the wind, the horses bore down on their prey, and it was then, to the amazement of everyone on board the cart, that the three horsemen drew long, glinting swords from their sides and charged violently towards the wretched, elderly man who had tripped and fallen headlong onto the sand!

The riders were almost upon their victim, when the cart jolted to an abrupt halt, the six Gargoyles released the poles and rushed across the beach towards the desperate quarry of the horsemen!

The horror-stricken man staggered to his feet, then fell again, his hands feverishly clutching at the gritty sand, as the horses were suddenly upon him.

He yelled unheard screams as their wild hooves pulped him into the soft seashore and deathly, silver swords scored the air just above his hooded head.

He knew that he had only moments to live!

His sand covered, cloaked body yielded and fell limp.

He gasped a final breath, and...

Then, a sudden roar from the charging Gargoyles filled the air like thunder! The horses' ears pricked up and their bulging eyes wildly stared at the rampaging, hideous creatures bearing down on *them*!

All three reared in alarm, their forward hooves frantically threshing the salty air, reaching for the screeching gulls that circled above!

The horsemen desperately fought to control their steeds, managed to rein them in, and then, amid a flurry of sand, flying spurs, whinnies, tossed manes and flailing swords, the horses galloped back across the rippled shore as fast as their hooves could carry them!

As they vanished into the forest, silence fell upon the churned sands, other than the cry of the gulls and the lapping waves.

The Gargoyles gathered around the wretched cloaked body and their captives in the cart stared at the sad dishevelled heap of rough cloth which seemed to have been washed up on the shore.

Then a miracle happened.

The cloak moved!

Just a small movement...no more than a twitch.

Another followed, then another!

Megan Magwitch yelled at the top of her voice, shattering the silence. "He's alive! He's alive!"

A moment later, she'd jumped from the cart followed by the rest.

They pelted across the sands, but the Gargoyles growled and blocked their way.

"Save him! Save him!" exclaimed Jessica, unable to burst through the solid barrier of stony muscle and sinew.

Then, amazingly, the monk began to struggle to his feet.

One of the Gargoyles, quite surprisingly, gently helped the elderly man as he stumbled dizzily towards the wagon, his aged face bruised and bloodied.

As he weakly climbed the steps he reached for something hidden deeply in the thick folds of his cloak.

"I bring you gold! I bring you gold!" the old man panted, and hastily produced a small, ornate golden coronet embedded with rubies, which he handed over to one of the Gargoyles.

"The rest of the gold has gone!" he gasped. "You are too late! King Henry's men have taken many a sackful, and the rest has been taken to the hills by my fleeing brothers! Haste ye back to the sea cave!"

The Gargoyles began to harness themselves back between the wooden poles and turn the wagon around so that it faced what Jessica and Jamie knew as Sandsend.

As the cart picked up speed across the sand, Lepho quickly discovered from the monk that the Gargoyles were desperate for more gold from

the Abbey so they could manufacture more of their "tempus crysta".
"Tempus crysta!...time crystal!" explained Lepho, as calmly and coolly
as he could without alarming everybody. "The Gargoyles have found a
way of changing the white crystal of their quarry into "time crystal" by
placing it next to the emerald and gold of the *Crown of Rasinja*! They
have found that if they can pass through a tunnel of such material, then
they can go *backwards through time*...and they need enough *time crystal*
to make the tunnel long enough to take them back ten centuries, a
thousand years, to the time when they plagued the Upper World!"

Jessica and Jamie, Jonathan and Jane and the
Magwitches stared at Lepho as he told the monk's tale. They just
couldn't believe what they were hearing!

Was it true, was it possible that they had actually travelled *back in
time nearly five hundred years* to the time when King Henry Tudor
was destroying the Abbeys of England? Had they really just witnessed
three of Henry's men about to kill an escaping monk?

So that accounted for the huge size of Whitby Abbey instead of it just
being a ruin...and there being no hotels on the clifftop...no road to
Sandsend...and no Sandsend!!

It was absolutely incredible!

But they had to believe it! They had just seen it all with their own
eyes!

"But will we be able to get back to the Twenty-First Century?...and
Christmas Day?....and Dad?" gasped Jessica, with the first hint of a
tear in her eye. "Of course we will!" insisted Lepho. "The power and
magic of *Aqua Crysta* will see us through all adversities!"

The elderly monk, who was called Leonardo,
immediately questioned Lepho about this *Aqua Crysta*, but Lepho
decided it would be better to suggest he found Old Soulsyke's well,
rather than invite him onto the return journey.

After all, he wasn't sure what the Gargoyles had in
mind, although at least he had found out from Leonardo why the

creatures had kidnapped Megan and her daughters in the first place. It was so that they had some people in human form to steal gold for them from the Abbey. Their idea had been to send the two daughters, and keep Megan as hostage near the sea cave to make sure they returned with the treasure. Now that even more Aqua Crystans had turned up in the shape of the four J's and Lepho, even more gold could have been stolen. But, as in even the best laid plans, something could always go wrong! In this case, the arrival of King Henry's men and their ransacking and destruction of the Whitby Abbey! And they, too, were after gold and jewels to fill the King's coffers!

Fortunately, for the Gargoyles, they had earlier befriended a solitary monk on the beach near the seacave and threatened that if he didn't fetch gold, then the Gargoyles themselves would destroy the Abbey. Leonardo's supply of trinkets helped in the production of *time crystal* but it wasn't enough. And as the *Crown of Rasinja's* power was beginning to weaken, the Gargoyles were becoming desperate. They needed still more green crystal to make their tunnel longer so they could reach even further back in time, and return to when they were banished from the Upper World.

      The cart eventually arrived back at the mouth of the cave, Jessica and Jamie still, of course, unable to believe what they were seeing...or rather not seeing!!

This was almost the very spot where they had built a sandcastle back in the summer! Up above should have been a car-park and then the disused railway line and the station. Now it was just bushes and trees and gulls wheeling and screeching in the air. When they looked back towards where the town of Whitby should have been, there was no road, no golf course, no distant hotels! But instead, there was the enormous Abbey towering above the cliffs, still magnificent despite the raging fire and the clouds of smoke which hung above it. The huge central square tower surrounded by tall, majestic arches was staggering to look upon, and they felt strangely privileged to be seeing it.

As the cart turned into the seacave, Jessica and Jamie glanced for one last time into the Middle Ages. The wheels came to a halt and Leonardo, after having said something to the Gargoyles, climbed down the steps onto the shingle.

He waved goodbye as he walked back onto the beach and Sixteenth Century England. Meanwhile the cart rolled on into the future. It was a strange feeling for everyone, and they all hoped and prayed that the tunnel would work in reverse!

As with all return journeys, it seemed much faster going back through the cave. The walls had dried out by now and all the passengers were thankful for there being less drips from the ceiling. In next to no time they had left the daylight and the roar of the sea behind and they were beginning to see the first streaks of green light from the tunnel ahead.

But as the passengers peered between the heaving shoulders of the three pairs of Gargoyles, they began to see long shadows in the distance...moving long shadows!

Figures came into view as the green brilliance began to make them shield their eyes. Through squinted eyes the passengers could make out trucks of green crystal and worker Gargoyles busily chipping away at the cave walls and then studding the crystals into hundreds of small holes.

Overseer Gargoyles watched the feverish work and barked and growled at any workers who slowed down.

The tunnel was rapidly being extended. The truck loads of green *time crystals* and all the Gargoyles must have been lowered down the shaft from the white quarry on the circular craft, using the great chain winch.

As the cart arrived at the entrance to the tunnel, the heat radiated even more strongly than before. The wheels slowed and then stopped as the way ahead became impassable. Overseer Gargoyles snapped and snarled at the captives and beckoned to them to climb down from the benches. Small metal pickaxes were thrust into their hands and Jessica, Jamie and the Aqua Crystans found themselves forced into the toil of extending the time-tunnel walls.

The heat was unbearable and unrelenting, as slowly but surely the tunnel was lengthened to twice its original extent, with the truck loads of crystal gradually being used up and embedded into the walls.

At last the slaves began fixing the one remaining heap of green crystals onto the cave walls. As they did so, one of the Overseer Gargoyles tossed Leonardo's golden coronet onto the pile. The effect was spectacular as the pale green crystals sparked and fizzled into brilliance. The magical chemistry the Gargoyles had discovered was truly amazing, and in no time these last lively time crystals had been fixed into the walls and ceiling.

The time tunnel was complete!

Exhausted, the captives were herded back onto the cart and this time six smaller worker Gargoyles were harnessed to the wooden poles and ordered to pull the wagon onward. The way ahead was now clear as the wheels rolled on and on through the crystal tunnel. The relief from the heat was very, very welcome, as the cart trundled through the last section of the crystal archway.

Soon, the green brilliance was left behind as the wagon rumbled along the rest of the seacave towards the bottom of the shaft which lead up to the quarry.

A sense of homecoming swept through the captives, although they knew at the back of their minds that the journey was not going to be easy, and worse, they all knew that they were still at the mercy of their monstrous captors.

On top of that they wondered whether or not they were back in the Twenty-First Century. Had the time-tunnel worked in reverse?

Or were they still trapped in the Sixteenth Century in these depths so deep beneath *Aqua Crysta, George* and *Deer Leap*?

They didn't have to wait long to find out!

Chapter 12

It was Melita Magwitch who heard the noise first... a thudding, clattering sound coming from the deep, distant darkness of the cave. A noise that could just be heard over the rumbling wheels of the cart as it trundled towards the shaft.

Louder and louder it became until the echoing din forced the hands of the passengers to their ears. Then the surging wave of sound swamped the cart itself as scores of moving solid shapes swarmed past them. Gargoyles, a bustling, torrential river of them, their grotesque outlines just visible in the dim light, all heading for the crystal time-tunnel! The evacuation of their realm had begun!

They were on their way into the depths of history, to the end of the first millennium, to a time before the invasion of William the Conqueror in 1066, another five hundred years before the destruction of the Abbey of Whitby!

On and on, the river of stone gushed by the fragile cart which had been forced to a standstill.

Then, as suddenly as it had begun, the torrent faded and stopped, the echoing footsteps vanishing into the distance.

Silence returned, save for the rumbling wheels as the cart continued towards the shaft.

"They're using the shaft to ferry themselves from the quarry!" Jamie suggested. "There must be dozens of them to come yet!"

He was right!

By the time the wagon had trundled another half mile, five more torrents of excited, wild Gargoyles had flooded round their wooden island, almost crushing and breaking it into pieces. How it survived the raging hordes no-one knew, but survive it did, and in the darkness of the cave, its eight buffeted passengers were relieved when what appeared to be the last swarming horde vanished into the distance.

It was then that the unthinkable happened!

Unthinkable but inevitable!

The six worker Gargoyles who had dutifully drawn the cart through the constant chaos unshackled themselves, and with a chorus of wicked, feverish cackles, followed their brethren back into the mists of time. They had obeyed orders, and taken the prisoners as far as they could, but now their instinct to be with their own kind forced them to desert the cart and its cargo.

Seconds later they had vanished.

Gone, the last of the Gargoyles! Forever!

With any luck, because of the ending of their quarrying and with it the heat generated around the *Crown of Rasinja,* things would begin to return to normal in *Aqua Crysta*, Queen Venetia would be safe, and the evil doings of the treacherous Tregarth would be exposed to all!

The weary passengers climbed down the ricketty steps and stood in the darkness of the cave.

It was then, with the total and complete silence all around them, that they began to realise that they were still far from home, and there was still one task to perform to ensure the Gargoyles never returned!

The destruction of the crystal time-tunnel!

It *had* to be done! Of that there was no doubt! With it still in place the Gargoyles could return to their quarry and even march on *Aqua Crysta* itself!

There wasn't a minute to lose! And it also suddenly dawned on them that the tide could rush up the cave from the sea at any time and drown them all!

It would take them a while to get back to the crystal tunnel and then there was the enormous task of removing all the crystals from the walls and ceiling!

They left the cart and began jogging along the cave. It was quite dry now and the going was easy, but as the green light began to gleam in the distance, they heard a new, high pitched tap-tapping sound clink-clinking from afar.

Jessica had visions of the Seven Dwarfs and Snow White, and the tune *"Hi -Ho, Hi-Ho, It's Off To Work We Go!"* kept tinkling away in her mind.

As usual, the same thoughts had occurred to her brother, and soon Jamie's attempts to whistle the song had everyone trying to join in. The Aqua Crystans had never heard the tune before, but soon they were all humming along especially the Magwitch girls. Jonathan and Jane had vague memories of the melody from when their nasty uncle listened to his radio back in the 1950s at Old Soulsyke Farm, and they, too, joined in!

The tune raised their spirits and all at once they found themselves almost at the beginning of the Gargoyles' crystal time-tunnel...but as they gazed into it, their whistling and humming stopped as though at the command of a hidden conductor.

Before them were the *Seven Dwarfs*!!

Or rather *six of them*!!

As they crept forward, they watched the six figures tapping away busily at the walls of the tunnel with hammers and chisels. Piles of loosened green crystals littered the floor. The speed of the work was incredible accompanied all the time by a constant pitter-patter of falling crystals.

"They're the six worker Gargoyles who pulled the cart!" whispered Jonathan.

But if they're destroying the tunnel, how are they going to go back in time?"

"They must be following orders!" sighed Jessica. "They've been sacrificed! They'll never see the rest of the Gargoyles again!"

"But what will happen to them, when they've finished their task?" asked Matilda, for the first time beginning to feel sorry for these sad remnants of the monstrous Gargoyles who had kidnapped her family. Moments later, Matilda had her terrifying answer!

One of the Gargoyles suddenly stopped his breathless chiselling. He had spotted his unwelcome audience.

A frenzied burst of desperate jabbering and cackling was followed by a scene that chilled the spectators to their very bones.

As though caught red-handed committing a crime, the Gargoyles, as one, dropped their tools with a discordant clatter...and then froze solid, unmoving, rooted to the tunnel's floor!

They didn't move again!

Somehow, each one's life had been ended by some mystical force. They were dead!

Each but a lifeless, cold statue!

Seconds earlier they had been a whirl of animated activity. Now they were mere stone!

The onlookers crept uncertainly into the remains of the tunnel, stepping carefully around the piles of crystal debris.

The walls, although deeply pitted with scores of roughly etched holes, were now similar to the walls in the rest of the seacave. The dead worker Gargoyles had chipped away at least three-quarters of the crystals, leaving still a broad arch of green at the far end.

"We will have to use their tools to finish the job!" said Jamie, a little hesitantly, as he edged round the first stricken statue. He was half expecting it to suddenly spring to life and grab him with its huge clawed hands...but nothing happened. They were well and truly dead. He even plucked up the courage to touch the second Gargoyle, its fearsome face frozen in anger. He gently touched its muscle-bound forearm. With a wince of pain he withdrew his finger as though a bolt of electricity had shot through it!

"It's like ice! Absolutely freezing!" he cried as he shook his hand vigorously, trying to restore its warmth. The coldness had almost bitten him with its ferocity. The pain was like that when fingertips ache with cold when bare hands have been digging in snow for too long. Excruciating! Tingling and throbbing at the same time!

No-one dared touch another as they made their way to the far end of the tunnel gathering the simple metal tools as they went.

Soon, the tap-tap-tapping of eight dwarfs could be heard, as crystal by crystal fell to the floor and the broad archway shrunk to a narrow band like a glassy, green rainbow. The task was almost complete.

"There can only be half a century or so left!" beamed Jamie, as he dislodged a particularly large crystal.

"It's the bit made from the last crystal load brought from the quarry - the load that Leonardo's coronet was thrown into!" said Jane.

"Poor, old Leonardo!" sighed Jessica. "I hope he's safe!"

"I wonder if he ever got to Old Soulsyke Farm and the secret well," said Jamie, as he chipped another crystal from the wall.

"I can assure you that he did!" Lepho said with a knowing glint in his eye. "He was a good friend of my father's. They were both..."

He was suddenly interrupted by a sound, a sort of whimpering sound, coming from deeper in the cave beyond the grotesque statues.

"What's that?" whispered Melita, pausing from her chiselling.

"Surely it can't be a Gargoyle!" burst Jamie. "One that's not dead after all...or one that's just pretending to be dead...!"

Once again, the whimper eerily crept upon them, this time a little louder.

Then, in the ghostly green light, they could see a shape...a figure...staggering and limping towards them.

"It's another Gargoyle!" gasped Megan, thinking another wild, swarming horde would be close behind.

As the solitary, rather bent and weary creature came closer, Jessica shouted excitedly,

"It's the injured one, the one we saw being beaten! He must have been left behind!"

But on hearing Jessica's sudden exclamation and seeing his dead comrades, the forgotten Gargoyle exploded into life and hobbled at top speed through the littered piles of crystals. On and on he went, weaving in and out of the corpses, flailing his arms wildly like a windmill, until he was level with Lepho.

Lepho tried to tackle him, but the panicking Gargoyle was unstoppable.

"Stop! Stop!" yelled Lepho. "Stop! Stop!"

A moment later the Gargoyle had plunged through the last remaining arch of the time-tunnel.

"We've got to stop him!" pleaded Jessica. "He thinks he's going to find the rest of the Gargoyles in the Eleventh Century, but he won't...he'll be sometime in the *last Century*!!"

With a surge of feelings of sympathy for the solitary, injured Gargoyle, Jessica dropped her tools and leapt through the crystal arch in pursuit of the poor creature.

"Jess, come back!" shouted Jamie. "Come back!"

"I've got to go after her!" he desperately called to Lepho.

Before Lepho could persuade him not to, Jamie had plunged beneath he crystal bow, and was gone!

"Stop!" Lepho called after them. "The tide will be upon us! We will all die if we don't get out of the cave!"

But his calls were unheard.

Although they could still be seen running into the distance, the two children were *half a century away*!!

Chapter 13

With his great steps and apparently untold reserves of strength, the Gargoyle made rapid progress through the cave. "We're never going to catch up with him!" panted Jessica desperately. "And even if we do, we're never going to be able to stop him!" gasped Jamie, feeling his legs turning to jelly with tiredness.

"But we've got to help him!" insisted Jessica. "If he suddenly bursts out of the cave into the *Twentieth Century* instead of the *Eleventh Century*, I dread to think what will happen! And besides, he'll be all alone and lost!"

The Gargoyle's determination was certainly matched by Jessica's. She had always been the same. Jamie knew perfectly well that whenever his sister got the bit between her teeth about anything...especially an injured or orphaned animal...there was no stopping her!

When they had lived in Scotland, she was always rescuing fawns and fox cubs and the like. She even managed to rear an abandoned owlet until he was able to look after himself. She'd called him Ozzie, but then everything got a name whether it was a snail or a stag! In fact, she'd once called a snail Brian...not after the snail in one her dad's favourite television shows, *The Magic Roundabout*, but after their postman!

Needless to say it didn't go down too well with the postman, who wasn't exactly like lightning!

Daylight gradually lit the way ahead, and the children could see that the Gargoyle was beginning to slow down, and take on the limping, bent posture he had had when they first saw him. Exhaustion must have finally overcome him as he staggered towards the mouth of the cave, hoping at any moment to be reunited with his fellow worker Gargoyles.

But instead, the pathetic creature just stood there, motionless, reptile eyes coldly gazing at the horrifying scene before him. A sudden burst of bright sunlight made him shield his hideous face, at the same time illuminating his worst nightmare.

Almost instantly he willed death on himself, as had his comrades in the time-tunnel. Death would mean escape and peace. Anything would be better than taking one more painful step into this living Hell!

But as much as he yearned for death's icy touch, it just wouldn't embrace him.

He tried and tried, but nothing would come. He was so weak and desolate, he couldn't even summon one last flicker of energy to end his life.

If he could have wept stone tears, he would have.

Jamie reached him first, carefully tiptoeing over the crunching shingle. The Gargoyle was so still that he thought he must be dead. He gently touched him on his stony wrist, expecting the tell-tale twinge of cold pain...but the wrist didn't feel like ice, it felt like warm stone. He was alive!

It was then that Jamie looked for the first time beyond the mouth of the cave, and saw what had so shocked and dismayed the Gargoyle.

He just couldn't believe his eyes.

"Is he alright?" came the distant, echoey call of his sister from deeper in the cave. "Please tell me he's not dead!"

There was no reply.
Her brother was as dumb-
struck and motionless as the
Gargoyle.
"Jamie, what's the matter?"
she gasped as she ran as fast
as she could into the daylight.
"What's happened?"
As her feet
crunched on the shingle, she
too, stopped and stared
beyond the mouth of the cave
and into the dazzling
brightness.

Slowly, she gingerly stepped towards the Gargoyle, his huge, broad,
muscled back arched beneath his sweeping stony mane.
Without any thought of danger she slipped her hand into his, feeling
the enormous, rugged palm, and the gnarled knuckles and claws.
Glinting above them was the thick iron band which had worn deeply
into his tortured wrist when he had been chained to his truck.
She felt his despair and as she glanced up at his saddened face, a tear
for him welled in her eye.
This was not the desolation of an ancient English
coastline he had dreamed about while toiling in the quarry. This was not
what the overseers had promised during those long, hard days when he
had dragged his truck backwards and forwards with load after load of
crystal. This was no reward!
Instead, what lay before him was a scene completely alien to his eyes.
Beyond the cave mouth, on the beach, totally
unaware of the three figures standing staring at them, were hundreds of
people!
Adults and children, all packed on the scorching beach, lounging and
playing in the blazing mid-day sun. Youngsters were busily building

sandcastles with moats and colourful paper flags sprouting from little towers.

Others were paddling and splashing in the shallow, rippling sea, while others delighted in jerky rides given by a team of saddled donkeys. Parents and grandparents were slumped in striped canvas deckchairs or laid out in the sun on tartan car rugs.

It reminded Jessica and Jamie of the day their dad had taken them to Sandsend just after they had arrived at *Deer Leap*. But, there was something different...odd...not quite right! The sun, the beach, the sea all looked the same...but somehow the people seemed different...not as colourfully dressed. The boys were wearing baggy, woolly, blue and black swimming trunks, while the girls were dressed in dull, one piece swimming costumes. Other boys wore baggy, light coloured trousers which were neither long, nor short, but sort of below their knees, while nearly all the girls had their hair in pigtails.

There were certainly no gawdy fluorescent T-shirts and shorts. There wasn't a pair of flashy trainers in sight. Instead were black school pumps and brown sandals. Some of the dads wore sleeveless pullovers and had their shirt sleeves rolled up tightly, almost up to their shoulders.

Some were wearing trilby hats and sucking on smoky pipes, while their wives wore longish, floral skirts and had strange wavy hair-do's.

Then a large white horse appeared pulling a two-wheeled cart, with a man in white delving into a tub and selling vanilla ice-cream cornets and ice-cream sandwiches between two wafers.

In no time, a queue of children and adults snaked across the golden sand, all eagerly looking forward to some cool refreshment on this scorchingly hot day.

"I bet Jonathan and Jane would have liked to have seen this!" whispered Jamie. "All the boys remind me of Jonathan somehow, with their khaki shorts and pumps, and sandals and long socks!"

"And the girls look like Jane, with their pigtails and plaits!" whispered Jessica.

"And I know someone else who'd like to here!" said Jamie with a grin.

"Dad, of course!" smiled Jessica. "It's all like the old black and white photo she's always showing us, of when he used to come here on his hols in the Nineteen Fifties!"

Just then, a trio of small children, none of them more than about three years old, suddenly came into this old picture postcard view.

Giggling and armed with cane fishing nets and buckets and spades, they started splashing in a shallow, clear rock pool just beyond the mouth of the cave. So captivated by their paddling and exploring, they didn't realise that just feet away, were three time travellers watching their every move!

Sandsend in 1954

117

One of them, a dark-haired boy, shrieked with delight when he saw a crab scurrying from under a rock. He quickly plunged his chubby fingers into the pool, caught it and waved it in front of the two blonde-haired girls. With a chorus of screams, both girls splashed out of the pool, turned and eyed the captured crab suspiciously. One of them was just about to cautiously walk forward and investigate, when she noticed out of the corner of her eye something far more interesting in the mouth of the cave!

She stopped and stared, unsure what to do next.

Her two companions looked up to see what she was gazing at...and then...in a flurry of arms and legs, and wildly splashing water...the little boy dropped the crab and sprung out of the pool as though he'd been stung by a jellyfish!

The three of them stared in shocked silence at the strange sight in the cave...two children with brightly coloured waterproofs and wellingtons, on a boiling hot day, and between them, a weird, stone statue, the like of which they'd never seen in their lives! The three in the cave stared back, and as they were wondering what was going to happen next...*it happened*!!

The Gargoyle suddenly shook his hand free of Jessica's and stepped forward.

The result was absolute and utter chaos!!

From the shocked, gaping mouths of the children erupted such an ear-piercing chorus of screams, that the whole beach fell into silence! Everyone stopped what they were doing and looked to the foot of the cliff.

Everyone!

Then, as if drawn by a gigantic magnet, they all flocked towards the trio of children who were rooted to the spot, not daring to move. The sea, the car-rugs, the deckchairs, the ice-cream cart were all deserted, as the startled holiday-makers rushed to the scene.

Some distance away, they all stopped and gathered in a strangely silent, inquisitive crowd, whispering to one another and pointing, trying to put a reason to this totally unexpected arrival on this perfect summer's afternoon.

Two men, with pink bodies and wearing nothing but billowing blue shorts and sandals and knotted handkerchiefs on their heads, pushed their way out of the crowd and shouted towards their children.

"*Jean!...Linda!*...daddy's here!" shouted one. "Just stay still! I'll come and get you!"

"*Neville*, don't move!" called the other. "Daddy'll have you out of there in no time!"

Gingerly, they both stepped forward, and walked calmly across the sand to the rock pool. The crowd gazed on in silence, anxiously watching their every step. They reached their children...and...then... in a sudden movement, they grabbed the three dumb-struck youngsters under their arms, ran back to the safety of the crowd, and handed them to their tearful mothers.

The people in the crowd started clapping and chattering with a kind of shared relief, but then, little Neville suddenly silenced them again.

"It's a monster!" he yelled, as loudly as he could. "It's a monster! It moved! *It was going to get us!"*

"It was going to *eat us!*" burst Linda.

"It was going to *eat us alive!*" echoed Jean.

The crowd, as one, gasped with horror.

"*It's from outer-space!*" called a bearded man in a straw hat.

"It's an alien, and it's captured *those* two poor children as *hostages*!!" called a plump lady with an ice-cream cornet. "We've got to do something!!"

Then, one hairy chested young man, with black, grease-plastered hair and clutching a stick of rock, boldly stepped forward in front of the admiring crowd.

Seeking glory and newspaper headlines, he strutted arrogantly towards the mouth of the cave determined to be the one who first spoke to the alien visitor from some distant galaxy.

But, whether or not it was the way he brandished the stick of rock, the Gargoyle, for some unknown reason, took exception to the young man, and took two giant strides towards him!

The crowd, as one, gasped, and took two equally large strides backwards, as the young man dropped the rock, turned and pelted as fast as his bronzed legs would carry him back into anonimity.

The Gargoyle, meanwhile, with recovered energy, bounded towards the astonished onlookers, who instantly scattered, screaming and running in every direction, leaving their belongings behind them.

Jessica and Jamie chased after him as he headed towards the narrow road bridge that spanned a small stream which flowed into the sea.

The holiday crowd was by now in a complete panic!

Parents grabbed youngsters up in their arms. Deckchairs, car-rugs and picnic hampers were abandoned. Even the ice-cream man deserted his horse and cart...and those who were lucky enough to be sitting on donkeys just kept on going towards Whitby!

The scene was one of utter pandemonium!

Once on the bridge, more chaos reigned as traffic screeched to a standstill. Morris Minors, Ford Populars, Rovers and Austin A30s ground to a halt, and their passengers hung out of the windows looking at the strange, hideous monster that stood on the little bridge. The driver of a blue and white Bedford OB bus honked his horn in the hope that the creature would shift pretty smartly.

He should have been in Whitby ten minutes ago, and he knew his Inspector would never believe his excuse of a monster on Sandsend bridge!

People in the little cafe under the railway viaduct choked on their sausage rolls and cups of tea as they stared out of the windows.

The owner quickly slammed the door, locked it and put up the closed sign, as if the creature might suddenly fancy a cuppa and a bite to eat!

The Gargoyle then headed up a steep, grassy bank to the railway line and the brick built station. Jessica and Jamie wove between the cars and followed him up the slope.

When they'd visited Sandsend during the summer, there certainly hadn't been a railway viaduct, but they remembered sitting on the platform of the disused station. Then the track had just been gravel, cinders and overgrown nettles and dog roses. But now, when they finally reached the top of the grassy bank, they could see a pair of shining railway lines bolted to their wooden sleepers.

And the station was now a smart, working building!

Tubs of bright flowers decorated the platform. Seats, with luggage piled next to them, stood in a neat row facing the line. There was a ticket office and highly polished brass oil lamps above maroon and cream signs saying *"Sandsend"*.

On a noticeboard, a colourful poster welcomed passengers to the "Beautifully Bracing Yorkshire Coast!"

The only thing missing were people on the platform! But having heard and seen the commotion down below on the beach and on the road, they

had all locked themselves in the little waiting room, leaving their luggage by the seats. They were all peering out of the windows, but the Gargoyle was nowhere to be seen.

Then, Jessica, having got her breath back, noticed him standing on the railway line, just at the end of the platform where the viaduct over the stream's valley began.

She could tell that he was as confused and alarmed as all the holiday makers.

"Dodo," she said in a soft voice, walking towards him.

"Dodo, everything's going to be alright! We've just got to get you back to the cave!"

Jamie, just behind his sister, looked at her in amazement.

"Dodo?" he quietly asked. "Who the heck's *Dodo?*"

"I've called him Dodo after the extinct bird," Jessica whispered.

"His species is almost extinct, except for him, so we've got to save him! OK?"

Jamie raised his eyes to the sky, shook his head and smiled knowingly. His sister was at it again! But this time with a creature a thousand years old!

Down below, the beach and the road were packed with people all straining their necks to catch a glimpse of the alien from outer-space! The metal and wooden lattice work of the viaduct hindered their view, but occasionally someone would shout out, *"There it is!"* or *"I can see it!"* or *"Try and get a picture for the papers!"*

As Jessica got closer and closer to Dodo, a hush fell upon the crowd.

Who was this strange girl in the wellington boots who seemed to be talking to the alien? They all watched intently wondering what was going to happen next.

Nearer and nearer, Jessica stepped with her hand out as a gesture of friendship.

"It'll be alright, Dodo, we'll look after you," she softly said. "You'll be safe with..."

122

But then, without a word of warning, the ticket-office door burst open, and a large, roundish man dressed in a dark blue uniform and peaked cap marched onto the platform.

It was Mr Simpson, the station-master.

His duty called, and whether there was a monster on the line or not, he just had to announce the impending arrival of the 1.19 from Whitby!

He raised a shiny silver whistle to his lips and the tense calm was suddenly shattered by a long and loud piercing whistle.

"The One-Nineteen from Whitby calling at all stations to Middlesbrough will be arriving in one minute!" he bellowed across the empty platform.

"And will the...the whatever it is...please get *off* the line??"

Then he marched over to the edge of the platform, and with clenched fists on hips, glared at the Gargoyle, Jessica and Jamie.

"You know it's an offence to loiter on railway proper...!" he roared, but he never got the chance to finish his warning.

From beyond the viaduct, came the tooting whistle of the 1.19 from Whitby and as its enormous, billowing cloud of smoke came into view, the viaduct began to shake and rattle!

Dodo looked panic-stricken as his body shook.

He turned and saw bearing down on him the great, gleaming black steam engine, hissing and puffing like another monster from the fiery depths of the Earth.

"Run, run, Dodo!! Run!!" shouted Jessica and Jamie, as the wheels of the engine spun and screeched, and skidded to a halt, just feet away from the bewildered and terrified Gargoyle.

Amid clouds of hissing steam, Dodo, at last, set off down the track, passing Jessica and Jamie and the dumb-struck station-master!

On and on he ran and then disappeared out of sight round a tree-lined bend in the distance.

Meanwhile, all the railway carriage doors on the train had swung open and the shocked passengers were climbing down onto the side of the track and making their way along to the platform.

"Ladies and gentlemen," shouted the station-master, "apologies for any inconvenience, but if you'll come onto the platform, the 1.19 will be ready to carry on to Middlesbrough in just a few minutes!"

Jessica, saddened by the thoughts of never seeing Dodo again and of what would become of him, walked gloomily back along the track.

"And I'd like a word with you two!" suddenly snapped the station-master. "Was that, that...that thing...with you?"

"Yes, *he was!*" snapped back Jessica. "And he's not a *thing*! He's called Dodo, and he should be back in the *Eleventh Century!*"

Mr Simpson removed his peaked cap, slowly scratched his head, and sat down on a suitcase. He looked around at the chaos on his prim little platform, shook his head and mumbled to himself. Was all this really happening?

Only ten minutes ago he'd been having a cheese and pickle sandwich with his wife. The day was bright. Everything seemed peaceful at his little seaside railway station. But then, his whole world had been turned upside down! Whatever had he done to deserve this?

Or, was it all one terribly nasty dream?

Jessica and Jamie sat on the edge of the platform, wondering what to do next. Should they go after Dodo, or make their way back to the cave and rejoin Lepho and the others in the future? They knew that Lepho wouldn't wait for ever.

"Come on, Jess, we've got to get back!" said Jamie.

"But what about Dodo? He'll be terrified!" sighed Jessica. "They'll hunt him down and show him to the World as a long lost monster or an alien from space!"

Suddenly, they heard a young voice behind them.

"He'll have gone in t' tunnel, just round yon bend!"

Jessica and Jamie turned and saw a pair of brown sandals, a pair of long, grey socks and a pair of tanned knobbly knees below a pair of baggy, khaki short trousers.

The young boy sat down between them and dangled his legs over the edge of the platform.

He looked at them both one after the other and smiled.

Both Jessica and Jamie thought his face seemed strangely familiar, but they couldn't quite think where they'd seen it before.

"Hello! I'm on holiday here," said the boy. "In one of the camping-coaches over there!"

He pointed to a couple of green and cream railway carriages standing on a short siding-line next to the station.

"M' name's Ted Dawson! Who're you?"

There was a stunned silence.

Jessica and Jamie both nearly fell off the platform with shock.

The boy was *their father*!!

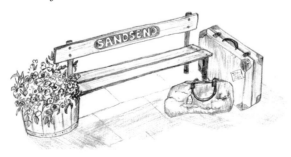

Chapter 14

It was true! He *must* be their father! This blue eyed boy with the pudding-basin haircut! The one they'd seen so many times in old, dog-eared photographs. It struck them both, of course, as they gawped at him with open mouths, that it *could* all be a coincidence. That this could be another Ted Dawson...not their father at all. But his appearance, together with the facts that this was Sandsend railway station and he was staying in one of the camping-coaches and it was the 1950s, all added up to him really being their father...years and years before he'd become a father!!

But before they could utter a word, another voice called out from the mayhem on the platform.

"Hey, you guys! May I have a few words with you?"

They turned to see a young man in a checked sports jacket emerging from the chaos, waving a notebook and pencil.

"I'm from the local paper, the *Whitby Gazette*. May I ask you a few questions?"

Ted quickly jumped up from the edge of the platform, dragging his new friends with him.

"Follow me! I'll save you the hassle!"

And, as though jumping to one of their father's commands, Jessica and Jamie quickly followed Ted through the platform hustle and bustle, weaving in and out of the bewildered passengers and passing the station-master, his head still buried in his hands, perched on the brown suitcase.

A couple of seconds later, they were darting up the metal steps of one of the smart, green and cream camping-coaches, just behind the station.

Ted slammed the carriage door shut behind them, and all three collapsed into an old, threadbare easy chair which was in the first room down the corridor...one of the bedrooms.

"You'll be safe here until all the fuss has..."

Ted suddenly stopped, and beat his fist on the arm of the chair.

"Darn it! I've gone and dropped m' new *Matchboxes* I've just bought in Whitby!"

He jumped up from the chair.

"You two stay here, while I go and look for them. They'll be on the platform somewhere!"

With that, Ted rushed out of the carriage, banged the door behind him and clattered down the metal steps.

Jessica and Jamie were left to gaze around the holiday bedroom of their own father, as a *boy*!

"This is absolutely amazing!" whispered Jessica, as, somehow, she knew she couldn't really be there. It was impossible! She hadn't been born yet...and wouldn't be born for another forty years!!

"Look, there's his fishing rod that's in the shed at *Deer Leap*!" she pointed out.

"And that's his cricket bat he has on his study wall, signed by his hero, Jim Laker!" gasped Jamie, pointing to the brand new bat lying on one of the empty bunkbeds.

There were *Dandy* and *Beano* comics scattered all over the place, all dated 1954, and a *Daily Mail* newspaper with headlines about the ending of food rationing in Britain and something about the Suez Canal.

"There was an eclipse of the Sun yesterday, according to this!" Jessica whispered, poring over the front page.

"This is really, really weird!" she went on. "Today's Thursday, the first of July, Nineteen fifty-four! I just can't believe it!"

Jamie had found an open shoe-box on the floor with several small metal toys inside, some of them protruding from small cardboard boxes. There was a single-decker bus, a green removal van, a caravan and a lorry with a small crane on the back and a few racing cars. They reminded him of the tin toys they had found in the forest cellar back in the summer, but these were a little more modern and certainly didn't wind up with keys.

"Dad's always on about the *Dinky* and *Matchbox* collections he used to have!" he said, picking up the removal van. "He reckons if he'd kept them, they would have been worth a fortune by now!"

Just then, the carriage door opened and Ted climbed glumly into the corridor.

"Did you find 'em, Da...Ted?" burst Jamie, quickly correcting himself.

"No, I didn't!" he replied sadly. "Somebody's picked 'em up and nicked 'em!"

"They'll turn up!" said Jessica, trying to look on the bright side.

"That's three shillings down the drain! Six weeks' pocket money!" said Ted, downheartedly. "They were wonderful...a red London double-decker bus 'n' a steam-roller!"

He solemnly came into the bedroom and sat on the edge of one of the bunk beds.

A brief awkward silence followed as Jessica and Jamie didn't really know what to say.

"Did you see the eclipse yesterday?" ventured Jessica a little uneasily.

"I did! It were brilliant!" replied Ted. "Did you?"

"N...no...we were, hmm..." mumbled Jessica.

She was suddenly saved by a loud knocking on the carriage door.

"Are you back from Whitby, Ted?" came an excited voice. "You've missed all the fun! Have you got your *Matchboxes*?"

"Who's that?" Jamie asked.

"Oh, it'll be Jonny from next door!" replied Ted, suddenly cheering up. "Him and 'is sister, Jane, come 'ere ev'ry year. Same time as us!"

Jessica and Jamie looked at one another in utter astonishment!

Now, not only had they met their own father, but they were about to meet Jonathan and Jane who should be down in the seacave with Lepho and the rest, waiting to return to *Aqua Crysta*!!

At that point things got a bit too much for Jessica. She stood up and grabbed Jamie's wrist.

"I think we'd better go now!" she said as she stepped into the corridor, pulling Jamie behind her. "Thanks for your help!"

"Anytime, it's been nice meetin' you!" said Ted. "You could've stayed 'n' 'ad a ginger beer w' us! I hope yon newspaper feller's gone! Oh, by the way, why are y' wearin' wellies 'n' them fancy macs on a day like this?

You must be boilin'!"

"Oh, we've just been exploring a cave," replied Jessica, looking a bit self-consciously at what she was wearing.

Ted squeezed through from the bedroom and stopped Jessica opening the carriage door.

"You don't mean yon cave at foot o' yon cliffs?" he asked with a note of urgency in his voice. "'Aven't you seen the sign, it's big enough?"

"No, what sign?" asked Jamie.

Another loud volley of knocks rattled the door.

"Hang on a min, you two!" Ted called through the little window, looking at Jonathan and Jane who were standing on the steps.

Jessica and Jamie, although not really wanting to, both looked, rather sheepishly, through the window at the visitors.

It was the Jonathan and Jane they had met in Pillo, both exactly the same as they were now...faces, clothes...everything!

"It says 'KEEP OUT! DANGER OF ROOF COLLAPSE!'" said Ted. "You couldn't 'ave missed it!"

With that, Jessica pushed the carriage door wide open, nearly knocking Jonathan and Jane off their feet, and darted at top speed across the platform.

The train, with all its passengers now on board, was pulling out of the station, with just the station-master standing on the platform with a green flag in one hand and a brown paper bag in the other.

As Jessica and Jamie waited impatiently for the last carriage to pass them so they could run across the line and down the slope to the beach, Mr Simpson suddenly shouted,

"Here, you two! Is this bag yours?"

Without stopping to think, Jessica grabbed it, stuffed it in her waterproof pocket and headed off across the line and down the grassy bank.

"Thanks, mister!" called back Jamie. "It's our dad's! We'll give it him when we get back! It's Christmas Day, you know!!"

"I'd like a word or two with *your father*!" roared Mr Simpson. "Where is he?"

"Right behind you!" shouted back Jamie as he disappeared down the slope.

The station-master turned round, and scratched his head again, as he looked at the boy with the pudding-basin haircut standing just behind him with a couple of friends.

He slowly shook his head, and plodded off to the ticket-office.

"What a day!" he mumbled to himself. "What a day!"

Jessica and Jamie didn't stop running until they had entered the cave. As Ted had said, the '*Keep Out!*' sign was indeed, 'big enough'!

It was huge!

"We've got to keep going!" panted Jamie. "We've got to take the risk, otherwise, we'll be trapped in Nineteen fifty-four for ever!"

After a brief pause for breath at the mouth of the cave, both of them jogged as fast as they could through the seacave. Deeper and deeper they ran.

The sound of the sea faded and the cave became darker and darker...until, at last, they could make out the faint green light from the remains of the time-tunnel.

Closer and closer they ran, their legs almost turning to jelly...and then, they could see, the crystal archway itself and the shapes of waving figures just beyond it.

It was then that they heard the roar!

The sound of thunder!!

"What's that?" screamed Jessica.

They both turned, while still running...and saw a dimly lit, enormous figure in the distance bearing down on them.

Another roar filled the cave!

"The roof's going to coll..!" shouted Jamie, breathlessly.

"It's *Dodo*! And he's dragging a *rowing boat*!" shouted Jessica, as the monster reached them, picked them up under one of his arms and carried on running towards the arch.

Then, with one final bound, Dodo leapt forward in time and collapsed exhausted onto the cave floor next to the amazed Aqua Crystans.

Lepho quickly freed Jessica and Jamie, while Megan and her daughters pulled the red rowing boat through the last arch of the crystal tunnel.

There was no time to lose. Already the tide could be heard pounding at the mouth of the cave. In next to no time it would be rushing and flooding upon them. The remaining crystals had to be removed from the walls as quickly as possible. Tirelessly, they all chipped at the green gems, until just three remained...then two...and finally the last crystal fell onto the cave floor. Jessica quickly grabbed it and placed it carefully next to the brown paper bag in her waterproof's pocket as a souvenir.

The past had vanished for ever!

Meanwhile, Dodo beckoned to everyone to join him in the boat.

No one was arguing!

They all clambered aboard, sat down and braced themselves for what was to come!

The journey home was about to begin!!

Chapter 15

In the dim green light cast by the myriad of fallen crystals, the boat's anxious passengers could just make out the first frothy wavelets of the approaching tide. The red wooden boat which was beached upon the smooth drifts of sparkling emeralds was suddenly engulfed by the tide's crawling fingers, and then lifted off the glassy reef.

"Hang on tight, everyone!" shouted Lepho, as the boat, at first, began to inch forward. Then, with an abrupt lurch, she was afloat and on her way.

Swirling seawater buffeted the flimsy vessel. She rocked from side to side. But, on and on, she was pushed like flotsam in the powerful current. Soon, the crystal drifts had been submerged and left far behind, as the boat plunged deeper and deeper into the darkness.

The passengers held on for all they were worth and just hoped and prayed that they wouldn't capsize or be overwhelmed by the water completely filling the cave.

Although there was no way of telling, the boat's speed seemed to increase, but then, to the horror of everyone, the rapid forward motion suddenly stopped!

"We're spinning round and round!" gasped Jane.

"We've been caught in some kind of whirlpool!" screamed Jessica, holding on to her brother and Lepho as tightly as she could.

"No, we've come to the end of the sea-cave!" yelled Lepho against the deafening roar of the sea beating the cave walls. "We're above the shaft's circular moving floor. Anytime now, we're going to start the upward journey!"

He was right.

The red boat slowly stopped spinning, and came to rest on the floor. Then, as the tidal force began to build up beneath it, the floor and the boat began to rise up the shaft. Still, all was dark, although one by one, those with the Queen's crystals delved beneath their garments and illuminated the familiar stony walls.

As they rose higher and higher, the greenish white disc that was the top of the shaft gradually formed out of the darkness. This time, it seemed to Jessica and Jamie as though they were approaching a distant planet. Brighter and brighter, larger and larger, the now silvery disc became, until they could make out the great cross beam with the chains winding over it.

Higher and higher they rose, and by now they could see the full spectacle of the Gargoyle's toiling labour - the enormous spherical quarry.

The greenness seemed to have faded.

The throbbing hum was no more.

As the circular floor came to a smooth halt almost level with the top of the shaft, Dodo gestured that the rest should follow him.

The Magwitches, then the four J's and finally Lepho stepped from the little boat while Dodo kept it steady. Then, as everyone made their way towards the giant crown, Dodo dragged the little boat behind him as though it were a toy.

The *Crown of Rasinja*, while still half buried in white crystal, was nowhere near as fiery and lively as it had been earlier. Before, sparkling, dancing flames had danced within its gemstones, but now its energy had died along with its heat and throbbing hum. The magical process that the Gargoyles had created had somehow ended after it had served its purpose. The Gargoyles had gone forever, so now the crown was just a crown, though a very splendid and enormous one indeed!

"What I can't understand is how it became so huge!" Jamie said as he stared upwards to the very tip of the green and golden mountain.

"I think," pondered Lepho, "that the Gargoyles discovered the mists that lap the spiral staircase near the *Star Cavern*. They must have found a way of hoisting the crown up to the end of the passage which overlooks the Cavern, and then taking it through the secret doorway and down the staircase."

"So, each time they did it, the crown would become bigger!" finished Jamie, with a beaming smile.

"But do you think it will ever give off so much heat again and affect the waters of the River Floss?" asked Jonathan.

"That, I cannot tell," replied Lepho, "but I am optimistic that it will no longer have a ruinous influence over our realm!"

The party, lead by Dodo, walked up the winding white track through the magnificent quarry. In contrast to their earlier visit, it was now eerily quiet and still. Gone were the hordes of worker Gargoyles and their brutish overseers. Discarded tools lay everywhere, together with the chains, trucks and whips of slavery. The beautiful crystalids still fluttered all over the vast quarry, their glinting colours making the place look like an upset, giant jewellery box!

Dodo looked sadder than ever as he thought of his missing friends somewhere back in the depths of time. He was alone, but at least the harshness and cruelty of his life was over.

The Aqua Crystans wondered what would become of him.

Would he travel with them to *Aqua Crysta*?

They thought not, as there, his never ending life would perhaps be dogged by his freakish appearance. He would never feel comfortable.

On the other hand, what was left for him here in the underworld? Alone in a deserted kingdom. Perhaps he would eventually be able to will his own death, like his comrades had done in the crystal time-tunnel.

Jessica, in particular, felt desperately sorry for him, especially because he seemed so keen to help them return to *Aqua Crysta*. Even now, he was securing the boat onto an abandoned truck with chains. He then beckoned his followers to climb aboard, and with a surge of great strength began to haul the strange vehicle towards the top of the white, glistening quarry.

Soon they left the gleaming whiteness, the crown and the crystalids behind and entered the gradually steepening cave which lead to the *Star Cavern*. The going was difficult. Occasionally the passengers had to climb out of the boat and help Dodo manhandle it and the truck through very steep and narrow parts. But, in time, they could see ahead of them the warm, red glow of the Cavern. The slope lessened and at last they entered the Cavern's vastness with its forest of red stalagmites.

The staircase was ahead, then the secret door and the passage that lead to the *Cave of Torrents*...and home!

With undying strength, Dodo hauled the boat and truck along the winding path through the mass of stalagmites. After passing the last one was the cave that held the entrance to the magical staircase.

Would they shrink as they climbed it?

Would the mists still have the power?

The same thoughts passed through the minds of each of the anxious travellers.

This was the moment of truth!

It was now...or never!

Calmly, when Dodo drew to a halt, they disembarked and looked apprehensively at the first few stone steps, the wooden handrail and the wisps of swirling mist that lapped them.

Dodo began to untether the boat from the truck. His intention was to carry the boat with him up the staircase as it would speed the journey down the *Cave of Torrents*. His confidence in the mists was infectious, and it was Megan Magwitch who stepped tentatively onto the first step, thoughts of *Torrent Lodge* spurring her on.

But, as her sandalled foot gently touched the roughly cut stone, she suddenly recoiled and screamed with horror!

For there, in a swirl of mist, on the fifth step, she had seen two black boots and the familiar hem of a dark purple cloak. More and more of the figure emerged as it slowly descended the steps. A knotted, grass woven belt.

A silver sword and a silver dagger.

And then, the face they dreaded seeing most!

The face of the man who would stop them returning to *Aqua Crysta*!

Chapter 16

There was no mistaking the evil, dark eyes which pierced them all from beneath those angry, knitted eyebrows. The grim set lips and the square, determined jaw said it all, as the menacing, towering figure stepped down from the last stone step.

It was Tregarth!

And, he was in no mood for pleasant greetings.

"So, we meet again!" his voice boomed through the cave. "You thought you had got the better of me, did you?"

From the staircase stepped two of his henchmen, dressed in hooded cloaks and carrying drawn swords.

Tregarth's voice dropped to a dangerously soft, mocking tone.

"Well, it is too late. I suggest you bow and pay your respects to the *King of Aqua Crysta*, King Tregarth!"

"Long live the King!!" chorused the two behind him, brandishing their swords.

"You lie, Tregarth!" roared Lepho, stepping forwards. "The Queen is still on her throne and you know it!"

Tregarth lifted his sword and thrust its deathly point towards Lepho's chin.

"You question my right to the throne?" demanded Tregarth, angrily.

"We all do!" shouted Megan. "Long live Queen Venetia!"

"Long, live the Queen!" chorused everyone.

The echoing exclamation rebounded through the cave, but as it faded, a far more sinister sound filled every nook and cranny.

A roar! A roar of such tremendous dimensions that the very ground shook and stalactites plunged to the cave floor. It was a sound that Jamie and Jonathan knew only too well. It was the sound of the monstrous reptile they had encountered when they had struggled to open the secret door! A sound of such ferocity, it was as though the whole realm of *Aqua Crysta* was about to come tumbling on top of them!

Tregarth plunged forward and grabbed Megan Magwitch. At the same time, his two cloaked sidekicks grabbed Matilda and Melita.

"Pay homage to your King, or they die!" yelled Tregarth.

At that moment, Dodo suddenly stepped from the shadows looking more hideous and fearsome than ever. He lunged his long, grisily arm at the tyrant and knocked the sword from his hand. Then he grabbed hold of him and swung him into the cave. Tregarth crashed heavily to the ground and rolled helplessly into the opposite wall. His terrified henchmen instantly released Matilda and Melita and fled up the staircase into the mists.

As another immense roar filled the cave, Dodo excitedly jabbered, *"Gargon! Gargon! Gargon!"*

Frantically, his face full of fear, he gestured to the others to climb the steps.

"Gargon! Gargon!" he repeated.

It was then that the red glow from the *Star Cavern* was almost extinguished, as the huge beast, Gargon, appeared by the last stalagmite, like some monstrous creature from pre-history. Its huge reptilian head swayed from side to side, as its ponderous, clawed forefeet crashed into the cave.

Panic stricken, the Aqua Crystans fled up the steps, followed by Dodo struggling with the boat.

On and on, the monster thundered into the cave accompanied by another horrifying roar.

Lepho lead the terrified Magwitches up the staircase into the safe, swirling fingers of the mists. Jonathan and Jane quickly followed, while Jessica and Jamie helped Dodo with the boat.

"Quickly!" screamed Jessica. "It's getting closer!"

By now, Gargon's serpent of a tongue was writhing and squirming along the cave floor, followed by its enormous scaly head. It had sensed blood. Jamie, struggling with the rudder of the boat, suddenly noticed a glint of silver from the cave floor, half way between the foot of the staircase and the unconscious Tregarth. It looked like a long flute which had fallen from the tyrant's belt when he'd tumbled across the cave floor.

Against all reason, Jamie *had* to retrieve it and to his sister's horror, he suddenly flung himself headlong into the cave and grasped the flute with the very tips of his fingers.

Gargon's demon eyes spotted the movement and like lightning the monster's glistening tongue slithered towards its prey!

As its dripping tip touched Jamie's arm, he rolled away, scrambled to his feet and darted to the staircase, his heart pounding in his throat.

At the same moment, Tregarth regained consciousness and his dazed eyes fell on the hideous, terrifying creature that was almost upon him! He struggled to his feet and staggered across the floor of the cave. But he was too late!

Weakened and numbed by his fall, he stumbled to the floor.

Gargon's tongue whiplashed towards the stricken, screaming traitor! Then, its squirming tip wrapped itself round Tregarth's leg. Two, three, four coils curled grotesquely up towards the impostor's thigh... and then, like a helpless fly, Tregarth was dragged towards the monster's gaping mouth...and, with a last, agonising scream, his arms threshing wildly, Tregarth disappeared between the rows of pointed, vicious teeth that lined Gargon's gaping, slavering mouth!

Jamie winced with horror, as the creature's huge jaws chewed on their captured morsel, whilst retreating backwards into the *Star Cavern*.

Then, with a silent prayer that the beast had been satisfied, Jamie clambered up the steps and joined Dodo and Jessica in the magic mists.

The nightmare was over.

Tregarth was dead.

Long live the Queen!

Chilled by witnessing the gruesome death of the treacherous Tregarth, Jamie joined his relieved sister in the lapping mists of the third step. She put a comforting arm around his shoulders, and together, with Dodo and the boat just ahead, they made their way up the winding steps.

As they climbed, the pink mists engulfed them, and they sensed the increasing size of the steps and height of the handrail.

Although they couldn't feel anything, they both knew that they were shrinking back to Aqua Crystan dimensions. Once again the steps and handrail gradually returned to their normal size, and it wasn't long before they could see their welcoming party on the rocky shelf at the top of the staircase.

"What of the villain, Tregarth?" called Lepho as the trio reached the last dozen or so steps.

"He's dead and *gone forever!*" replied Jamie triumphantly, as though he'd slain the traitor himself.

The Magwitches burst into excited chatter, although they were still a little suspicious of Dodo.

"Queen Venetia will be absolutely delighted!" exclaimed Megan, hugging Jessica and Jamie, as they finally reached the platform.

She then noticed what Jamie was clutching in his hand.

"Tregarth's wood and silver flute!" she gasped with amazement. "How did you come by that!"

"He lost it when Dodo threw him across the cave, and I just got it before...!"

"Don't remind me!" shuddered Jessica at the thought of her brother's foolish heroics. "A second later and you could have landed up in Gargon's belly!"

Jamie smiled a little guiltily, and lifted the beautifully ornate and slender instrument to his lips and blew across the mouthpiece.

Not a single sound came from the flute.

He tried again, this time arranging his fingers to play a different note. But, once more, the instrument remained silent.

"Well, that was a waste of time!" Jamie sighed. "I risked life and limb for a duff flute!"

Lepho and the Magwitches all suddenly burst out laughing.

"You have earned a great trophy!" beamed Megan. "Your 'duff flute', as you call it, is...or rather, was Tregarth's greatest pride and joy!"

Jamie quizzically inspected the gleaming instrument.

"You mean, Tregarth's greatest pride and joy was a flute that doesn't play a single note?" he asked.

"That's just the point!" continued Lepho. "It's a silent flute to us, but the creatures of the Upper World can hear its songs perfectly!"

"So Tregarth used the flute to speak to the animals of the forest?" gasped Jamie, suddenly realising the magic power that was in his hands.

"That's terrific! I can't wait to try it out! Come on, what are we waiting for? Let's get the door open!"

It was then that they all noticed two cloaked figures slumped at the far end of the rocky shelf. Tregarth's two sidekicks.

"They are dead," said Lepho, in sudden solemn tones. "They have taken poison, either because they couldn't muster the strength to open the door, or they couldn't face returning to *Aqua Crysta*. Whatever the reason, we are well rid of them! Come, let us make haste!"

Dodo had already found the ring embedded in the floor of the shelf, and, inch by inch, with a loud grating sound, the vast triangular slab of rock was edging towards them. Soon, it gaped wide open, and as the Gargoyle strained on the taut chain, everyone slipped through the gap. Dodo kept on pulling and pulling and the gap was soon wide enough for the boat to be dragged through into the passage. When it was finally on the other side of the door, Jessica rushed back to Dodo to signal to him to stop pulling on the chain...but what she saw made her heart sink!

The chain was already winding itself back into its hole...the door was closing! Dodo had vanished!!

"Dodo! Dodo! Where are you?" she called desperately.

But the Gargoyle had gone.

This was the limit of his world. He couldn't go on. He had made the decision to return to what he knew, rather than face the unknown. He would probably will himself to death eventually, and the Gargoyles would be totally extinct...in the present World, at least.

Heartbroken, Jessica looked for one last time down the staircase and then ran through the closing crack, tears welling in her eyes. She felt that she had lost a friend.

In the passage Megan consoled her with a friendly hug, as the huge door finally grated to a halt and closed fast.

"But what about Gargon?" she sobbed, as Jane and the Magwitch daughters comforted her as well.

"The Gargoyles have probably lived with the perils of the monster for time eternal," explained Lepho gently. "Dodo, as you call him, will survive for as long as he wants to."

"But he could have lived in *Aqua Crysta*," sighed Jessica. "I'm sure he could. I feel so sorry for him all alone."

Jessica could suddenly stand it no longer. She suddenly brushed aside all the sympathy and bolted along the passage as fast as she could.

"Jess! Come back!" shouted Jamie, thinking of the first time he'd seen Gargon's fearsome head, as he and Jonathan had struggled to open the secret door.

But nothing could stop her and a moment later she was teetering on the very edge of the passage's end and staring into the bright red vastness of the *Star Cavern*.

Jamie rushed after her and tightly grabbed her hand. Together they looked down upon the distant stalagmite forest and its weaving paths, both of them hoping for just a glimpse of Dodo. But all was quiet and still. No signs of prehistoric monsters, no spine chilling roars, no throbbing hums from deep crystal quarries...no Dodo.

It was simply just the spectacular sight, with the shimmering, rosy red, crystal Cavern walls and the breathtaking, dizzy heights of the roof-clinging stalactites. They took in as much as they could and then turned and walked sadly back to join the others.

But, no sooner had they taken half a dozen steps, when they heard a familiar noise!

A jabbering clicking sound, echoing throughout the Cavern!

"It's *Dodo*!" exclaimed Jessica, excitedly rushing back to end of the passage.

Jamie followed, and together they peered down to the Cavern floor.

And there, in the middle of the stalagmite forest, was the lonely, castaway Gargoyle, gazing up at them, stiffly waving his stony arms and jabbering away in his own strange language, with friendly, twinkling crystalids fluttering around his head! Jessica and Jamie waved back, as Dodo began to walk towards the cave that lead back to the white quarry.

Lepho suddenly appeared between the two children, putting his hands on their shoulders.

"He's saying '*farewell*'", he whispered wisely. "He's saying '*goodbye*'!"

They watched him plod boldly along the path, and then with a final wave, he vanished into his underworld, gone forever.

The three of them turned, tears in all their eyes, and walked along the passage to join the others.

With cheerful thoughts of home dispelling the sad ones, the party of adventurers hoisted the little boat above their heads and marched along the passage. Soon they could sense the sweet aromas of *Aqua Crysta* tickling their noses, and with increasing excitement they could hear the watery roar of the *Cave of Torrents*.

Louder and louder the roar of falling water filled their ears, until suddenly they emerged from the dim passage onto the rock-cut balcony and looked in awe at the wonderful sight before them.

Not only was it beautiful, but it was home!

Torrent after torrent stretching as far as they could see!

The noise was deafening as they made their way down the steps and behind the greatest torrent of them all.

With a struggle, they managed to push and shove the boat down the narrow steep path, all of them now soaked to the skin. Thankfully, the hot, sticky, sultry heat had gone, so with a great joyful awareness of the final lap, they carefully set the boat in the river and prepared for the final voyage.

With everyone aboard and Jamie and Jonathan manning the rudder, the little red boat steadily glided out from the shore and into the main current. Wavelets bobbed her up and down and then, without a word of warning, she was embraced by the powerful flow and whisked off towards the first torrent.

"It's not quite as smooth as the *Goldcrest!*" laughed Jane, as they sped bumpily along, spray in their faces.

Everyone hung on tightly as the boat approached the first plunge. Laughter and chatter faded as nearer and nearer she sped towards the gurgling, frothy, first waterfall, Jamie jokingly adding to everyone's slight nervousness.

"*Five!...four!*" he shouted from the helm, "*three!...two!...one!*"

Then, like some fairground white-water ride, the prow of the boat dipped sharply, the whole vessel bucked, everyone yelled and screamed, got drenched...and the bobbing boat carried on as if nothing had happened!

On and on the voyagers braved torrent after torrent, laughing and screaming all the way. It was certainly the ride of a lifetime. Everyone was soaked, but they all thoroughly enjoyed it and thought it a fantastic reward for all the perils and hardships they had endured.

All was going well, until, suddenly, after the umpteenth waterfall, Megan noticed something strange ahead. She wiped her streaming wet hair from her face and squinted through the spray,

"*Torrent Lodge, ahoy!*" she called, in a tone of happiness and curiosity mixed into one.

It was true. *Torrent Lodge* was, unmistakably, straight ahead, but there was something peculiar about it...something very, very peculiar, indeed!!

Chapter 17

All eyes were fixed on *Torrent Lodge* as the boat plunged over the last and smallest waterfall before the Magwitch's stumpy stalagmite home. Its rounded smooth dome of a roof shone in the crystal light. Its little square windows and large curved door almost smiled a welcome. The whole place looked like a friendly, bald-headed dwarf....as it usually did. But it was the amazing decorations that made it different!

Hundreds of tiny, triangular flags of every colour imaginable festooned the house, all tied onto great lengths of knotted thread which wound round and round the outside of the stalagmite. It was as though it had been tied to a chair by hostile Red Indians! Two sagging rows of flags even crossed above the river from the lodge to the opposite bank!
It was a wonderful sight, and the Aqua Crystans gradually began to realise what it was all about. And, so did Jessica and Jamie.

It reminded them of the greeting they had been given when they'd arrived at Jonathan and Janes' house back in the summer. It was an Aqua Crystan welcome, but hardly ever used because newcomers were so rare.

As Jamie and Jonathan guided the boat into the shallows, it strangely all began to feel very eerie. Despite the great splash of colour, all was silent except for the sound of gurgling water behind them.

The boat glided onto the sandy shore.

Lepho climbed out and pulled her onto dry land, and one by one, everyone disembarked and made their way across the soft sand towards the smiling house.

Then, suddenly, from nowhere, a horn sounded a single note, long and shrill...the front door opened...and out stepped the slender, tall figure of Queen Venetia herself, her golden cascade of hair flowing from a silver coronet over a long, kingfisher blue gown.

With arms outstretched, she stepped forward, her face wearing the widest smile Jessica had ever seen!

Her band of loyal venturers were staggered by the sight, even the usually unruffled Lepho, who offered a mumbled greeting.

"Your Majesty," he began. "Your humble servants return, the quest accomplished! The *Crown of Rasinja* is safe! Tregarth is dead!"

As if in celebration of the wonderful news, another note from the hidden horn filled the Cave, and this time, what followed once more amazed and surprised the returning travellers.

From the Cave's every nook and cranny, from behind every crystal boulder, from every window of *Torrent Lodge*, beaming faces appeared! Score upon score of purple cloaked Aqua Crystans, and moments later, a deafening, joyous chorus of cheering and singing began!

The happiness and relief of every Aqua Crystan was undisguised. They rushed forward, encircling the bemused wanderers. Hands were shaken and warm, embracing hugs abounded as grateful thanks were expressed by everyone.

Welcoming speeches were made by the Queen and by Merrick, the ancient, snowy haired Mayor of Pillo. Then, a feast to end all feasts was held as tables of food and drink were set up in honour of the heroes.

Tales were told of underworld exploits and discoveries. Dodo was toasted with upheld goblets and tankards of bramble wine, and Lepho was presented with the glittering chain and medallion of *Deputy Mayor of Pillo* as reward for leading the expedition. He, in turn, thanked Jessica and Jamie, Jonathan and Jane and the Magwitches for their role in the historic venture, and then finally called for three resounding cheers for the Queen.

As the last and loudest cheer echoed through the *Cave of Torrents,* the tables were cleared and the long procession of Aqua Crystans began to weave along the narrow path to the River Floss. Farewells were exchanged with Megan and her daughters, and soon *Torrent Lodge* was returned to its accustomed tranquility, with just the sound of gently tumbling water for company.

With a flurry of final waving arms, Jessica and Jamie rounded a bend in the path and the Magwitches and their gaily bedecked home vanished from view. Along with Jonathan and Jane, they tagged themselves onto the back of the winding procession.

"What a welcome that was!" enthused Jessica, as she listened to the constant singing and chattering that was going on ahead. "You lot certainly know how to put on a party!"

"I've never known anything like it to be honest!" said Jane.

"Well make sure you let us know when the next one is!" laughed Jamie. "That food was fantastic! The Queen must have known we'd be absolutely starving!"

"Wasn't she delighted with Lepho's news?" said Jane, thinking of the Queen's beaming face. "It must have been a great weight off her shoulders!"

"I think the downfall of Tregarth was a great weight off everybody's shoulders!" remarked Jonathan, as he tossed a pebble into the river.

"And what a way to go!" Jamie said with relish. "You should have seen him disappear into Gargon's...!"

"OK, OK, little, nasty brother!" Jessica interrupted. "Besides, it's not only Tregarth's death that has cheered everyone, it's the return of cooler air to *Aqua Crysta*, now that the Gargoyles have stopped their quarrying and messing around with the *Crown of Rasinja!*"

It was true. The hot, sticky atmosphere had vanished and it was so refreshing to breathe in the normal sweet smelling, pleasantly warm air.

"I just hope the snow isn't too deep for us to get back to *Deer Leap*," said Jamie, thinking of the journey home through the forest. "At least the melted bits made it easy before!"

"I wonder what time it is up there!" Jessica suddenly thought, feeling a little guilty. She hadn't thought much about Christmas for what seemed like ages.

"It should be the same time as when we climbed down the well," said Jamie.

"But what about the time we spent at Sandsend?" said Jessica, anxiously, "Perhaps that'll make a difference! Perhaps it's Christmas morning and dad thinks we've been kidnapped or something!"

"Well, there's only one way of finding out," insisted Jamie, looking up at the roof of the *Cave of Torrents*. "The sooner we get back to *George*, the better!"

Despite the long queue for the *Goldcrest* at the end of the *Cave of Torrents,* the new Deputy Mayor of Pillo made sure that he and the four J's were among her first load of passengers. By now, all the houses at the junction hamlet were full again of happy, smiling Aqua Crystans. Miller Knapweed and the rest all waved as the ship glided smoothly away from the small quay, and Jessica couldn't help thinking about the last voyage she'd made...in the little red boat which they'd left on the shore at *Torrent Lodge*. And that made her remember Dodo who had, in the first place, dragged the boat along the seacave from

Sandsend and through the remaining archway of the crystal time-tunnel. As she leaned over the golden prow and felt the spray of the Floss in her face, she sadly wondered what Dodo was doing at that moment in his lonely underworld, way beneath the celebrations which had just honoured him. If only he could have been there.

In next to no time, Captain Frumo was ordering the *Goldcrest's* great, square yellow sail to be rolled away so that his ship could slow down and be guided steadily towards the pebbly shore from which Jessica and Jamies' red scarves soared up into the swirling mists of the Cavern roof. Scary memories flooded back as they remembered the moment they had jumped down from the well's last rung and been captured by Tregarth's grim faced, iron fisted henchmen. But as they recalled that terrible beginning to their adventure, they felt the hands of Queen Venetia and Lepho on their shoulders.

"Before we say farewell," began the Queen, quietly, "I would just like to thank you once more for your heroic deeds. When you arrived here your names were hated by many, but now they are praised by all, and will be *forever!*"

"And we hope," said Lepho, with a smile, "that we will see you again under pleasanter circumstances!"

"We hope so, too!" beamed Jamie. "Believe it or not, we've enjoyed every minute!"

"Well, *almost* every minute!" smiled Jessica, hugging first the Queen and then Lepho.

Then after exchanging farewells with their great friends, Jonathan and Jane, the two heroes made their way down the wooden plank onto the shore.

Amid much cheering and clapping, Jessica and Jamie walked over the white pebbles to one of the dangling red scarves. Already a piece of wood had been knotted into it near the end for the children to sit on.

Like last time, Jamie would be hoisted up first and then Jessica.
A group of Aqua Crystans took hold of the other scarf and marched
across the shore until it was stretched taut.

Jamie climbed aboard, slightly anxiously, but nowhere near as
nervously as he had been last time. This time he was confident that the
journey into the mists would work, and that he would soon be hanging
onto the well's last rung, full Upper World size, and awaiting his
sister.

With a last wave from Jamie, the Aqua Crystans
began to heave on their scarf.

Slowly, but surely, Jamie began to rise away from the excited onlookers,
the bobbing *Goldcrest* and the River Floss.

Up and up he floated, gripping tightly onto the fluffy red wool between
his hands, his wellington boots dangling freely.

Up and up, further and further away from the shores of the River Floss.
He glanced downwards and saw the magical world of *Aqua Crysta*
seeming to shrink before his eyes. Soon, the Floss was but a trickle, no
one could be seen and the Goldcrest had disappeared.

He took one last look at the wondrous, fabulous crystal Cavern and
then the first fingers of mist swirled round his mop of ginger hair.
He could see no more as he was enveloped by the mystic clouds, and
moments later he was stretching his hand upwards to grasp the metal
rung at the bottom of the well.

Quickly, he pulled himself up, made himself secure,
and began to tug on the scarf to let the Aqua Crystans know that he
had arrived.

Then he carefully threaded the scarf with the seat back down to his
sister.

The clouds, like last time, were invisible from the well and as he gazed
downwards he could see no sign of anything other than a tiny trickle of
water no wider than his thumb.

When the knot joining the two scarves was resting across the last
rung, he climbed the next two steps and waited for Jessica. He felt

no different but he knew he had grown back to full size. As he hung suspended between the two worlds, he wondered when he would see *Aqua Crysta* again. Already he could hardly wait!

Pictures of the Queen, Lepho, Mayor Merrick, Jonathan and Jane, the townships of Pillo and Galdo flashed through his mind as he hung there. Then he thought of the busy railway station at Sandsend, the three children paddling in the rock pool, Whitby Abbey burning fiercely and Leonardo, the monk running across the sands chased by King Henry's men.

It all seemed so unreal and so far away. In depths so deep...so much deeper than even the last time they had visited.

As he watched, the scarf began to move over the last rung. His sister was on her way!

Just moments later, the vivid, magical pictures dancing through his mind suddenly ended as he saw a familiar, scarlet, woolly bob-cap, copper hair and green waterproof emerging from the void and a hand grasping the metal rung below his feet.

Jessica, too, had arrived back in the real world. Or was this the imaginary world, and what lay below the real one? There was no way of telling!

With heavy hearts they silently wound in the two scarves and began the climb up the rungs of the well. Each, as usual, knew exactly what the other was thinking. They were both somehow unhappy at leaving the beauty and friendship of *Aqua Crysta* behind. They both had a yearning to live there permanently...but they knew such thoughts were wrong.

They belonged to the Upper World...to its beauty, to *Deer Leap* and their father. They would soon shake off their secret wishes and be as happy as ever, once they got back to the cottage. Or would they?

The question niggled away at them as they climbed, but gradually thoughts of Christmas Day with dad started to cheer them. As they passed the ledge that lead to the forest cellar, Christmas Day excitement was already beginning to grow in them.

It seemed to be drawing them upwards with a magical power all of its own!

Their hearts lightened.

They would soon be home.

Their real home!

Jamie reached the stone slabs at the top of the well which they'd left slightly apart. A snowflake landed on his freckily nose.

"It's still snowing!" he exclaimed, as he peeped through the gap. "And it's still night-time!"

He pushed one of the slabs upwards until it fell over softly, compacting the snow on the forest floor. He then scrambled out of the well and reached down to help his sister. A couple of minutes later they'd closed the well's secret entrance, covered it with grassy turf and snow, and were ready to trudge across the forest back to *Deer Leap*.

The snow began to fall heavier and heavier and they were already looking like a pair of snowmen.

"It's going to take us an hour and a half at least to get back with the thick snow and having no torch!" sighed Jessica with a shiver. "And it's s..so c..cold!"

Jamie, too, was beginning to feel the coldness of the night.

Before, they'd both been boiling when they'd first arrived at the well, with all the heat rising from *Aqua Crysta*, but now they felt chilled to the bone.

It was freezing!

"Hang on!" said Jamie, suddenly trying to find something beneath his waterproof. "I've got an idea!"

"What, you've got a couple of hot water bottles hidden under there?" Jessica asked with a shivery grin.

"No such luck, sis!" Jamie smiled, with snow clinging to his face. "But I've got *this*...!"

Chapter 18

With the flourish of a magician producing a wand, Jamie drew his prized possession from the inner pocket of his waterproof.

His hard won trophy from the underworld...Tregarth's wood and silver flute!

Like a buccaneer with a glinting scimitar, he swished it through the air and then brought it swiftly to his lips.

"Jamie!" exclaimed Jessica. "You *do* realise that I'm standing here freezing, don't you? Do you *really* think that it's the time and place to suddenly show off your musical skills?"

Taking not a scrap of notice of his sister's protests, Jamie blew gently across the slender flute's silver mouthpiece.

And just like the last time he tried, not a sound could be heard. Absolute silence!

"Come on, Jamie!" pleaded Jessica, impatiently. "You're not the Pied Piper! Put it away and let's get going!"

"Wish, Jess, wish!" whispered Jamie.

"I wish you'd get a move on!" snapped Jessica. "I wish I was in my cosy bed!"

"No, wish for *Strike* to appear!" Jamie whispered.

"Jamie! I think it's all getting too much for you! What are you talking about?"

"Just wish, that's all!" insisted Jamie. "You wish and I'll play and wish!"

"For the last time, little brother! If you don't come now, I'm setting off alone! Anyone would think we were in the middle of a fairy ta...!"

Suddenly, she stopped...her mouth fell open...and she stared hard over her brother's shoulder and into the dimly lit, snow laden trees.

"Jamie, Jamie, look, look!" she gasped in a loud whisper, hardly able to believe her eyes!

For there, standing in silhouette against the snowy forest floor, was a solitary deer.

"It can't be!" whispered Jamie, as the young roe deer took three or four steps towards them.

He blew again across the silver mouthpiece and the deer's ears twitched in the silence.

"It's *Strike*!" burst Jamie in as quiet a voice as he could manage. "It's *Strike*! He must have heard the silent flute!"

It was, indeed, the same deer that had carried them across the forest what seemed like ages ago. As he nimbly, and almost tamely, walked up to them, they could see strands of cut grassy thread around the base of his short, velvetty horns. The thread that had bound Jonathan and Jane while he had wandered the forest on the orders of the tyrant, Tregarth.

With no signs of fear, Strike allowed Jessica and Jamie to climb onto his back, and then, as though magically commanded, he sprang forward into the forest and headed towards Old Soulsyke.

Snow fell incessantly, as the ghostly deer leapt over countless white drifts of pine needles and countless remains of crumbling, stone walls.

Soon, they were climbing the small hill which was crowned by the ancient ruined farm.

It now looked more than ever like a giant Christmas cake, with the branches of its surrounding oak, beech and walnut trees piled high with snow.

There were no signs at all of any long corridors of melted snow and bare, brown forest floor. All was white.

On and on, Strike leapt across the woodland snowscape with the children hanging on tightly.

They passed by the small quarry and the old barn, and moments later they arrived at the perfectly round clearing where it had all began...*The Dell*.

Strike gently came to a halt and Jessica and Jamie calmly slid off him into the knee-deep snow. The tops of their two rocky seats were just about visible. The last time they had seen the boulders, the two rocks had been dripping with melted snow and surrounded by an island of brown forest floor with its strange, warm, hovering mist.

Jessica turned to pat Strike's head...but he'd gone...vanished into the forest... just like the last time. His duty done again.

The two of them stood there in the silence, giant snowflakes tumbling all around.

The magic was over!

Or, was it just beginning!

It was Christmas Day after all!

"Race you home!" shouted Jamie, excitedly.

They both plunged along one of the white corridors between the spruce trees, and were soon running through the gap in the hedge and into the cottage garden.

Breathlessly, they quietly shook off their wellington boots in the back porch, and hung up their warm woollies, waterproofs and scarves. But just as Jessica put her scarlet bob-cap on its hook she noticed five tiny shimmering droplets of glassy violet and turquoise tucked into the wool where it folded over to make a brim. Carefully, she picked them out one after the other and placed them on the palm of her hand. They were like tiny, crystal sweets with lots of glistening faces and edges dancing in the light and were almost transparent. Each was like a small tube, no larger than a fingernail and rounded at each end.

Jamie looked at them closely.

"I bet they're crystalid eggs! Remember, one took a fancy to your hat! It must have reckoned it was the perfect place to lay a few eggs! Keep them safe somewhere, you never know what might happen!"

Jessica stared at the tiny gems, thinking of the amazing possibility that they might even hatch! Baby crystalids! A brand new species in the Upper World! No, never in a month of Sundays! Things like that never happened.

Still, she carefully put them in her pyjama pocket and was determined to look after them. She even imagined five beautiful, fully-grown crystalids fluttering round and round in her bedroom...and her hero, Sir David, sitting on the bed trying to make a TV film about them!

The two of them crept through the kitchen and glanced at the colourfully lit Christmas tree in the front room. Jessica nudged Jamie as she looked at the clock on the mantlepiece, its fingers shining red in the glow of the lights.

It was just after two o'clock in the morning!

They had left *Deer Leap* only an hour earlier!
What an incredible night it had been!

And what an incredible day was to come, as
Jessica carefully placed under the Christmas tree a crumpled brown
paper bag on which she had quickly written:-

"To Ted, Lost and found
July 1st. 1954"

As they silently tip-toed up to bed, carefully avoiding
the third step from the top, of course...neither Jessica nor Jamie could
hardly wait to see their father's face later that morning.

The special magic was over...but another sort was just
about to begin!

GOLDCREST SHOW OPENS

Captain Frumo opened the 247th "Goldcrest Exhibition" to coincide with the Pillo Wine Festival. The vessel is in superb condition with the bows, oars and main mast having been re-gilded during the Upper World winter. Queues of Pillo Folk were all keen to see the work and to inspect a show of paintings by Galdo artists Pixwith Stem and Charles Underhill which are displayed in the cargo hold. The views of Aqua Crysta are excellent and well worth seeing.

NewArtForAll

The new art of painting is catching on all over Aqua Crysta. Since Pixwith Stem and his friend Charles Underhill developed the new pigments made from materials from the Upper World, it seems that everyone wants to have a go.

A current showing of the work of the artists is being shown at the *Goldcrest Exhibition*, and already many folk have started painting themselves, using the new pigments, brushes and paper developed by Stem and Underhill.

The two artists intend to hold demonstrations at Galdo, Pillo and Middle Floss after the busy Harvest season, but at the moment they require workers to help produce brushes etc at their workshop in Middle Floss.

New Crystal Vein Discovered

Pillonians are celebrating due to the accidental and totally unexpected discovery of a new crystal vein linking the quarry and Merrick's Ledge.

Master Carver, Elfrin of Pillo, said, *"This is one of the best ever veins ever found in the Kingdom and will yield some of the clearest crystal ever quarried. I can hardly wait to get my hands on it and carve my first chess set. It should be brilliant!"*

The vein, known as *Fryo's Vein* after its discoverer Fryo Pilsden from Merrick's Ledge, is easily workable as it leaves the quarry and across the Floss at the Ledge outcrop, but impossible to work in the Cavern roof of course. *"There will be a time when we can work the high ceiling of Floss Cavern, but it will be long after I am gone!"* said Elfrin, *"If only we could reach all that wonderful untapped crystal!"*

199TH SANCTUM CHAMPIONSHIP

This Harvest's Championship will be held in the Toadstool Forest and Picnic Spot at Galdo. Queen Venetia will be opening the 199th event at third high water. Twice champion and present title holder Hiolle Twig will be hoping to retain his title for a third time to equal his father's record run of wins set over a hundred harvests ago.

'My father, Folf, was a good teacher and I'm hpoing to put the Twig name back in the record books!' said Hiolle as he prepared for this Harvest's competition.

160

Queen Venetia Opens New Larder Cave

Yet another Harvest Season is upon us and to mark its beginning, Queen Venetia has opened the New Larder Cave at the top of the Harvest Passageway Steps.

Manager Gwillum Tadwin, eldest son of wine-maker, Liffy Tadwin, said, *'We're expecting more fruits from the Upper World than ever before to be collected during this Harvest so the new cave is an absolute necessity. It will have more capacity than any other Larder cave, mainly due to the removal of over one hundred 'tites and 'mites. We very much appreciate the skills shown in this operation by the quarrymen of Merrick's Ledge and the Heights of Serentina."*

Lepho is expected to be leading the first party into the Upper World within a a while or two. Outlookers have reported from the Forest and say that branches are heavily laden with fruits and nuts and that the fungus spread is excellent.

All of us at the "Crystal Times" wish this season's Harvest Parties the best of fortune.

TELLTALE QUENTIN A BIG HIT

"Quentin's Tales" is still going well in the Meeting Hall Cave. The run has been extended due to popular demand, although shows will have to be reduced during the Harvest.

Quentin, himself, is amazed with the response to his talks which tell the story of Aqua Crysta's eldest citizen. *"Folk seem to be captivated by tales from the past Upper World centuries. I'm sure that nearly everyone in Aqua Crysta has been to the show and some more than once!"*

According to Quentin, the tale that captivates folk most is the one in which he tells of his meeting with Jessica and Jamie from the Upper World when they first arrived in our Kingdom.

The show is booked up for a while, but tickets can still be obtained from the wine shops in Pillo, Galdo and Middle Floss

PILLO WIN REGATTA

There was much cheering and back slapping when *Pillo* managed to pull off a close victory in the most hard fought *Galdo Regatta* for many harvests.

The event was held during twelve successive high waters from the Galdo Falls with the home team scoring a creditable 125 points. but the visitors amassing a winning 135 points.

Captain of Pillo. Sylvan Underdown. was delighted with the result.

"It was the new event - the doubles nutshell relay - that swung it for us!" he said jubilantly after the cup presentation. *'We were determined to win it after all the practice we had put in back at Pillo!'*

161

a letter from Jessica

Hello again!

Well, it seems like it was only yesterday that I last wrote to you, but it was way back in late summer! Today's Boxing Day and what a Christmas it's been! It all started a couple of days before we broke up from school when Jamie and I were in the Christmas Concert in front of all the parents. It was the 'Pied Piper' and I played the old Mayor of Hamelin (I looked a bit like the Mayor of Pillo down in Aqua Crysta! You remember Merrick with the big white beard - a bit like Santa Claus!!) Jamie played the Chief Rat - a very suitable role, as he had to keep eating cheese and scaring the audience!

Of course, the best thing about this Christmas was our second visit to Aqua Crysta. We had a great time, although it was pretty frightening at times, especially on the beach near Sandsend when the knights were attacking the monk, and meeting the Gargoyles and then when Jamie tried to reach Tregarth's magic flute with that Gargon monster closing in on him. He must have been crazy! But travelling back in time was fantastic!! To see Whitby Abbey as it used to be 500 years ago and Sandsend beach on that hot summer's day and, to top it all, seeing dad as a boy with his Matchboxes! You should have seen his face when he opened that brown paper bag yesterday morning! He just cannot understand it! He never stops talking about it - and he actually remembers losing them and all that fuss on the station fifty years ago because of some strange creature, although he didn't actually see it at the time! Poor old Dodo! I hope he's OK down there. Somehow we've got to meet him again!

Dad liked his presents and I liked all of mine especially a set of story books and a new old-fashioned ink pen. Dad says its for writing stories in exercise books - he got me six of those, too - just to start me off, he says! Since I've been at the school here, I've never written as much! I think Aqua Crysta has inspired me!

But my favourite and most treasured things I've got have to be all the items I've brought back from our adventures - the quint and minstrel from summer, and now a piece of time-crystal, Queen Venetia's crystal, jay feathers and, of course, the crystalid eggs! Or that's what we think they are! Everything is tucked away in my bedside drawer, but its getting pretty full!

We had a great Christmas Day - our first at Deer Leap. We all did our bit when it came to the Christmas dinner. The pudding I made with Jamie was pretty tasty, although dad nearly choked on a £2 coin Jamie had put in it! I think he'd heard at school that coins are put in Christmas puds to bring luck or something!

By the way, Harry the Hedgehog is still with us! He never really became strong enough to let free, and he's just hibernated in a box of straw in the garden shed. Perhaps he'll get stronger next year. Since I wrote to you last we've looked after three injured deer - roe deer, a bit like Strike - and a crow with a broken wing called 'Knapweed', after Miller Knapweed in Aqua Crysta. I have often wondered why he grinds crystals! What do they use crystal dust or powder for? I wonder! I shall have to ask Lepho the next time we visit!

It's stopped snowing at last, and its really very deep. Dad says it's a good job we've got plenty of food. We'll never be able to drive into Goathland to get supplies! Still, we're all nice and snug here indoors, but we're looking forward to a snowball battle this afternoon and I think we'll have another go at building a couple of snowmen! Let's hope they don't melt like Bill and Ben did at the Dell.

Anyway, bye for now. I think I'll start writing a story in a crisp new exercise book with my new ink-pen! Now what can I write about? 'Crystal Dust' perhaps, a ship called the 'Goldcrest' and a Queen called Venetia! There's certainly plenty there to be getting on with!

bye,

love Jessica

a letter from Jamie

Hi,

Hope you've had a great Christmas. This one has definitely been my best ever, especially our second trip down into AC. It was really brill going back in time and seeing Whitby Abbey as a huge building, not a ruin like it is now. And the fun we had in Sandsend on the railway station with Dodo! Wow! That was fantastic! And meeting dad as a boy with his cricket bat and his toy cars. The flute I brought back is now safely under my bed. Still haven't got a single note out of it - and Strike hasn't turned up as far as I know! It's easy to learn how to play and it doesn't annoy anyone!

Christmas Day was super. I got some more models to put on my shelf and some plastic kits to build myself. One is of George Stephenson's 'Rocket' - one of the first steam engines, and the other one is of 'HMS Endeavour' one of Captain Cook's ships that took him to Australia. Incidentally, sometimes a full-sized replica of the 'Endeavour' comes into Whitby harbour and stays for a while. Try and get on it if you can, it's really cool! And don't forget to have a trip on the North Yorkshire Moors Steam Railway, too. That's ace! Oh, and I got a remote control racing car as well. That'll be great in the garden when the snow clears - although I hope it stays for a bit longer. Can't wait to pelt Jess and dad with snowballs!

School's been great this term. I'm in the football and chess teams and I was in the Christmas play - 'The Pied Piper'. I played the Boss Rat and had to scare everyone in the audience by belting up and down the aisles squeaking with a huge cardboard piece of cheese under my arm.

One of the other things I brought back from AC was my shrunken torch, when it fell over the end of the passage into the Star Cavern. It's tiny, no bigger than a paper-clip! I'll have to get a new one before we go to AC the next time. I can't wait to see Lepho and J and J. I just hope we don't land up locked in a dark cell again - that was the worst part of our last adventure...or was it being captured by the Gargoyles?
Or coming face to face with Gargon?
Have a happy New Year!

See you,

Jamie

164

a letter from Jonathan and Jane

Dear All,

We both hope that you enjoyed your Christmas festivities. We've never ever known an Upper World Christmas Day - our miserable uncle never bothered at Old Soulsyke and since coming to Aqua Crysta, every day has been like Christmas - not that we have days and nights, of course! Folk here are always giving presents and we seem to celebrate things all the time, especially when the Floss changes direction and the Pillo Falls come to life! According to Jessica, I think we seem to care more about our surroundings here ...the water that gives us long life, the crystals that give us light and lots of beauty, and, of course , all the plants that grow in the Harvestlands that give us food and drink.

We are both getting better at playing Quintz and Sanctum, mainly because of our neighbours Elfrin and Tilly. And would you believe it? We've started a cricket team here in Pillo! The folk from Galdo came to watch us play recently and now they want to have a team! Soon we'll have a match between the two sides. The Meeting Hall Cavern will be a great spot to play it! We already have Quintz and Sanctum competitions, and there's the Harvest Regatta for rowing teams, too!

We're both very glad that things have returned to normal here. It was becoming very, very hot and uncomfortable, especially here in Pillo, although we believe that the heat became unbearable inside the Island of Galdo. And to think that it was freezing in the Upper World with really deep snow. We've forgotten what snow is like, and most Crystans have never seen it!

Can't wait to see J and J again! We'd like to see Deer Leap. Perhaps J and J will take us there one Upper World day. We'd have to travel in their pockets again! We could see all Jamie's models and explore Jessica's bedside drawer where she keeps all her treasures! Hope this letter reaches you up there!

love from Jonathan and Jane

AQUA CRYSTA
Part 3

**If, once again, you've been drawn into
the magic of *Aqua Crysta* and would like
to visit the mystical realm for a third time,
watch out for:**

'FOREVER CRYSTAL'

It is the following Spring and strange happenings lead
Jessica and Jamie to a sad event in the depths of the Forest.
Once again they become involved in a quest to help
Aqua Crysta, this time encountering the
Guardian of the Crystal of Eternity himself, and the very
origins of the powerful magic that lies within the waters of
the enchanted, subterranean Kingdom.
Explore the amazing Needle Crag Cavern, with its ancient,
sinister twin sisters and their hideous, scheming butler, Grizel.
Travel by day on the *North Yorkshire Moors Steam Railway*
and by night in the talons of an Eagle Owl.
Meet a magical nightingale, a miniature Arabian stallion,
Lucius the Alchemist, and see how a gang of deer poachers
in the Forest come to a very sticky end!

Aqua Crysta   Part 4   StoneSpell

MOONBEAM PUBLISHING
P.O. Box 100, Whitby, North Yorkshire, YO22 5WA